Here in the Dark

for Joe,
with love,

Meagan Lucas

Advanced Praise

Here in the Dark
stories

by Meagan Lucas

"Honest and unflinching, elegant yet brutal, Meagan Lucas illuminates the darkest corners of the human condition in this extraordinary collection. These are stories wrought with sympathy and pitch-perfect realism, exploring the heartaches and hard truths about addiction, class, gender, and the perils of parenthood. Like Claire Keegan and Dorothy Allison, Lucas renders characters with a breadth of range but never fails to show a mother's love to these damaged souls. *Here in the Dark* is the declaration of a considerable talent."

—**Peter Farris**, award-winning author of *The Devil Himself*

"Meagan Lucas's *Here in the Dark* features strong, desperate, determined female protagonists, all fighting their good fights. The collection as a whole works like a murmuration, with characters all linked to their hard-scrabble Appalachian lives. This is Grit Lit and Rural Noir at its best."

—**George Singleton**, author of *You Want More: Selected Stories*

"Like lightning, every story in Meagan Lucas's new collection is a flash of brilliance - a bolt right to the reader's heart. With *Here in the Dark*, Lucas takes risks and never flinches, she embraces the darker sides of humanity, without once dehumanizing her characters and proves, without a doubt, why she's one of the most exciting new voices in Appalachian Noir."

—**Steph Post**, author of *Miraculum*

"Meagan Lucas's *Here in the Dark* is powerful and poignant. The 16 stories in this collection are full of heart and hurt and horror, each one illuminating her darkened corner of rural America in unflinching, unvarnished prose. Her characters are wounded but surviving, their hometowns ravaged but resilient, their stories painful but beautiful. This a necessary, unforgettable book about people and communities most often forgotten, from one of the finest Southern literary authors writing today."

—**J. Todd Scott**, author of *The Flock*

"It's obvious why Lucas and Shotgun Honey are a perfect match. Her stories are tightly wound coils of fury that push you into dark places just to pounce. This collection is a cherry bomb in a mailbox just waiting to blow your fucking fingers off."

—**Brian Panowich**, author of *Bull Mountain*

"Meagan Lucas's *Here in the Dark* is a superb collection of dark, gritty fiction in which womanhood takes center stage. Packed with tension and as many great last lines as there are stories, this is Lucas at her best, and the result proves she's as good at short fiction as she is at writing novels. Don't miss it."

—**Gabino Iglesias**, author of *The Devil Takes You Home*

"Meagan Lucas is one of the most exciting new voices in Southern fiction. In *Here in the Dark*, she crosses deeply nuanced portraits of compromised characters with genre-smashing narrative techniques, producing a collection of stories as exciting to read as they are beautiful and true. This one is something special."

—*Nathan Ballingrud*, author of *The Strange*

Here in the Dark

stories by

Meagan Lucas

SHOTGUN
HONEY

2023

Some of the stories in this collection have appeared elsewhere:
"Voluntary Action," Still: The Journal, Fall 2018 (Pushcart Nominated), "Picking the Carcass," Jacked: An Anthology, Run Amok Books, July 2022 (Pushcart and Crime Writers of Canada Excellence Awards Nominated), "The Only Comfort," Pithead Chapel, November 2021, "Buttons," Cowboy Jamboree, May 2021 "Sitting Ducks," Bull Magazine, February 2022, "Kittens," Santa Fe Writers Project, Issue 11, Fall 2017 (Winner of the 2017 Scythe Prize), "The Monster Beneath," It Came from the Swamp Anthology, Malarkey Books, February 2022 "Glass Houses," Change Seven Magazine, April 2022 (Best of the Net and Pushcart Nominated), "Hell, or High Water," The New Southern Fugitives, April 2018 "Porch Light Salvation," The City Quill, May 2016, "Frogs in a Pot," Storgy Magazine, January 2021, "And Then the Forest Will Burn Down," Passengers Journal, September 2022.

Published by **Shotgun Honey Books**

215 Loma Road
Charleston, WV 25314
www.ShotgunHoney.com

Cover by Bad Fido.

First Printing 2023.

ISBN-10: 1-956957-20-0
ISBN-13: 978-1-956957-20-4

9 8 7 6 5 4 3 2 1   23 22 21 20 19 18

For Josh, with love.
(Sorry there's no zombies.)

Contents

Here in the Dark

Voluntary Action

A river of sweat ran down Candice's back. She could feel it pooling beneath her breasts, and under her arms. Her clothes clung. The scent of vodka seeped out of her pores. Her thighs stuck to the vinyl chair. She was going to leave a sweaty splotch, in the shape of her undercarriage, on the seat. She wished she'd worn pants. Her lips were chapped and peeling, and she could feel the scratch of the dried flaps. She pinched the dangling skin between her teeth and pulled. A throat cleared. Not hers. Her eyes slid over to the investigator.

"Do you have a response, Ms. Nix?" he said, leaning forward.

He was clicking a pen with his thumb and Candice had no idea what the question was.

"Um…" she said, alternately searching the stained ceiling tiles and her fingernails for the answer.

He looked up from his notes. He would describe himself as a young fifty, Candice thought. His suit was nice; it hugged his shoulders. She felt wrinkled and damp. She couldn't remember the last time she wore this dress, any dress, really. He had salt and pepper hair trimmed short on the sides, left long enough on the top to sweep over. He got it cut somewhere hip. Not Great Clips, like her.

"I asked if you think Sherri Thompson deserves justice."

"Of course." Candice replied, pushing her frizzy bangs out of her face.

"Do you think her family, her children, deserve to know why she died?"

Candice nodded, and began to chew on the side of her thumb. The tip of her tongue worried a hangnail and she tasted blood.

"Ms. Nix, you're going to have to answer aloud." He tipped his head to the video camera in the corner. "This protects you and me," he'd said, setting it up, what seemed like hours ago.

She took a deep breath. "Yes."

"Isn't this important to you?"

"I'm sorry." She sat up straight. She tried to focus on his questions, but he kept asking about Sherri Thompson and Candice had spent every moment of the last three months trying to not think about her.

"Are you responsible for her death?"

There it was like a shit on the floor; the question that internal affairs, that everyone, wanted the answer to.

She blew out a breath. "I don't know."

"Why don't you tell me what happened, from the beginning."

"I wasn't feeling well…"

• • •

Candice's stomach heaved and vomit splashed into the gas station toilet. This morning's Bojangles sausage biscuit floated like rafts on the brown froth. Chunks of grape jelly dotted the jetsam. She rested her sweaty cheek on the cool plastic of the toilet seat and focused on breathing through her mouth. The repeated tap-tap-tap of a timid knock on the bathroom door broke her concentration.

"Candice," came a voice from the other side then a throat clearing. "Excuse me, um, Deputy Nix, we just got a call from dispatch."

The pile of toilet paper she'd placed on the floor crinkled

beneath the knees of her uniform pants. She stood as he tapped on the door again.

"Alright!" she called. "Jesus Fucking Christ, hold your goddamn horses."

She gathered the paper and mashed it into the overflowing trash can. She flushed. She washed her hands and ran them over her face. She accidently saw herself in the mirror. She looked like the stuffed toy her dogs dragged around the backyard. Her hair was dirty. She smelled like a hamster cage. Purple bags hung from her lower lashes and her cheeks were puffy. She looked at least fifteen pounds heavier than she was. She grabbed her thermos and opened the door.

January sky hung thick above the mountains on the horizon. It would snow tonight, if not sooner. Deputy McKenzie stood three feet from the door zipping and unzipping his coat. Hovering. She crossed the icy parking lot towards her cruiser and he followed in her wake.

"I can... um, drive if you don't feel up to it," he said.

She snorted. "Get in." She opened the driver's door and sat in the seat molded perfectly to the shape of her large ass. She crammed the key in the ignition. McKenzie had almost folded his lengthy body into the car before she started rolling, "Where to?"

He relayed the address from his note pad. "Blue Gap Road between Berea Chapel and Marshall Pass. Parole violation. Heroin. DSS is on the scene."

"This is some first day you're going to have." She took a deep drink from her thermos, the warm liquid calmed her. Hair of the dog.

"Why do you say that, the opioid crisis?"

She looked at him: hard bodied but soft cheeked, "You like sobbing kids?"

"Oh."

She ran her hand over her sweaty face and sighed. "Right. It's a crisis now. I forgot...now that the drugs are in neighborhoods with sidewalks, streetlights and fucking PTA." Candice took another drink and they passed a boarded-up auto body shop, and a ma and pop furniture place that was now a consignment store. "No one cares about our shitty schools, no jobs, good people trying to live off fucking disability and the poor drowning in their own vomit, or stroking out in their trailers. Darwin, they say. They buy stock in check cashing and title loan places, and grab up all the foreclosures. It just pisses me off that all of a sudden it's a crisis because some kids with money, with daddies who wear white shirts and ties, kids with futures, are dying. Dying is dying man. It's always a fucking crisis."

Candice watched the pavement fly under her tires. Rogue snowflakes stuck to her windshield. She sent a silent prayer to whoever would listen that it would hold off until the end of her shift. The mere threat of snow was enough to panic people and empty stores of bread and milk. By the look of the sky, she knew that the shelves at Ingles would already be bare. An inch or two meant that life for normal people ground to a halt. But there were always dummies who thought that the black ice was no match for their lifted truck. And then there were those whose needs, for liquids or powders or pills, drove them out into the weather, and ultimately into Candice's life. This month she'd spent more time squinting through her windshield and pulling idiots out of the ditch than anything else; her soon to be ex blowing up her phone with pics of the kids making a snowman or pelting the side of the house with snowballs without her.

She turned right onto Blue Gap Road, and looked at McKenzie. "You sure you heard that address, right?"

"I'm pretty sure."

"I don't think there's a house there. If I remember correctly that's the backside of the Gentry place on the one side, and state land on the other."

"Maybe you're thinking of someplace else."

"I've lived here my whole life."

Blue Gap narrowed after Berea Chapel and Candice eased off the gas. They both searched the banks for a break in the brush that would indicate a driveway, and potentially a house. Sure enough, they rounded a bend and a fresh driveway appeared. The gravel was still loose.

"What's the name?" she asked.

"Sherri Thompson."

"Shit." Candice banged her palm off the steering wheel. "I bet anything that's Sherrilyn Gentry. We went to school together." They pulled up in front of a single wide and parked behind a beat-to-hell brown Aerostar minivan and next to the navy Suburban DSS drove. The yard was spotted with mounds of dirt waving flags of brown grass and faded plastic toys. "I thought she went away to college."

As Candice and McKenzie climbed out of the cruiser and adjusted themselves, the front door opened. Five kids between the ages of ten and three coursed out, followed by a thin grey-haired woman with a toddler on her hip. As they marched closer, Candice could see their wide eyes, wet cheeks and runny noses. A medium sized one in the middle sniffed loudly. Candice looked over at McKenzie out of the corner of her eye. His adam's apple kept bobbing and his face was pale. The social worker nodded at Candice as she passed.

Candice walked toward the door. She heard the beep of the suburban unlocking, murmurs and a loud hiccup from the children. She hurried up the cement block steps and knocked on the door. There was no answer. She looked at McKenzie. He would never be ready for this, and it wasn't just that he was young and pretty. There was no way one could prepare themselves to take a mother away from her children. She knocked again and called: "Sherri, we're coming in."

She pushed the door open and stepped through. The floor was littered with toys and small socks. Papers with crayon scribble were taped to every wall. Two sippy cups and a plastic bowl with soggy cereal and thick milk lay on the scarred coffee table. Elmo sang a song on the television. The air was solid with the scent of other people's bodies, other people's food. Her stomach rolled and forced bile up her esophagus to remind her that it hated her.

"Where is she?" he asked, gun in hand.

Candice shook her head. Why one of these couldn't go smoothly, she didn't know. "They always go back to the bedroom." She signaled for him to follow with a jerk of her head. They moved slowly down the hall toward a half-closed door. Candice rested her right hand on the gun on her belt as she pushed the door open with her left.

Sherri was pacing on the other side of the bed. Her hands were in her stringy blonde hair. A men's undershirt and sweatpants dangled from her skeletal frame. Candice put her hands up.

"Hi Sherri. Do you remember me? I'm Candice Nix, well, I was Candice Hawthorne. We went to high school together."

Sherri glanced at them before turning and pacing away. The floor, bed, and every other horizontal surface was covered in trash or clothing.

"Sherri. We need you to come with us. You're going to need something warmer on though. It's cold out there."

Sherri didn't react, or stop moving. Her hands shook.

"She's high as a kite," McKenzie whispered, eyes wide.

"Yes. Watch carefully."

"Sherri." Candice said, hands still up, moving toward the strung-out woman. "Sherri, have you eaten?"

The woman paused and looked at Candice as if for the first time. "I'm hungry" she said.

"Let's go get you something to eat then," Candice grabbed a hoodie and a pair of sneakers from the floor as she guided Sherri out to the living room. She handed the items to McKenzie. "Put these on her." Then she went to the kitchen and pulled open the fridge. Finding nothing but a bottle of ketchup and some beer, she turned and surveyed the counter. She sighed and returned to the living room.

"We'll have to go through a drive-thru."

"That's not protocol."

"It's a small town, McKenzie. And it's a half hour drive into Asheville. She's obviously high, let's get her some food and she'll feel better. Why the fuck isn't she dressed?" McKenzie worked on Sherri's shoes while Candice pulled Sherri's damp arms through the sleeves of the sweater.

"You're gonna get hypothermia, girl. All this sweating."

They locked the door behind them and led her to the cruiser. Snow was beginning to fall in earnest and Candice had to use the wipers to clear the windshield. Hot air blew through the vents and fogged the windshield. Candice watched Sherri pull at the neck of her hoodie through the rear-view mirror. The hot air made Candice's head swim and her stomach turn, she dialed it down and slid her window down a crack.

"Is this what you were imagining?" she asked McKenzie. "Back in school? Is this the kind of police work you thought you'd be doing? Me, I pictured myself in a uniform, god the uniform is sexy isn't it? I was gonna help kids cross the street. Make these people feel secure. Help in emergencies too, right? Car accidents, or old people having heart attacks or breaking hips. I would have dreams sometimes about finding a piece of evidence that the detectives missed at a crime and getting a moment of glory. I never imagined this. Hauling girls I knew once to jail on drug charges. Pounding on doors to investigate reports of gunshots to find children home watching their baby brothers and sisters, diapers smelly and saggy, while Dad who hasn't had a job in years is out back doing who knows what, and Mom is at the diner pulling a second shift, again. I'll admit, Mayberry tricked me. Fucking Andy Griffith. I was fooled. Damn it." She punched the steering wheel. A chill ran over her skin and her upper lip was wet. Breathing deep to control the nausea she watched the road carefully for somewhere to stop.

Candice pulled into McDonald's parking lot, opened the door and threw up on the pavement. "I'm gonna go to the bathroom, and get her a burger. Watch her." She said at McKenzie and dragged her feet across the collecting snow. The bathroom was blissfully clean. Candice emptied her already empty stomach into the gleaming bowl, just bile now, bright yellow. She went to the sink and splashed water on her face. She put her hands under the air dryer to direct some of the breeze at her face and collar. She was damp and itchy. At the counter she ordered a burger and an orange soda and waited while a teenager in the corner watched her, or rather her uniform with hard eyes. She scowled at him as she carried her paper bag and cup out to the parking lot.

McKenzie was standing three feet outside the door, playing with his zipper again. His hair was full of snow. "She was screaming," he said.

Candice could see the cruiser bouncing from across the lot. The food made a wet thud as it hit the ground.

Candice ran.

Opening the door to the backseat she saw the stain on Sherri's pants and thought she'd peed them. It took Candice a moment to realize that it was sweat. "Turn the fucking heat down," she barked at McKenzie, ducking inside the car. Sherri was vibrating. Her skin was searing under Candice's fingertips. White foam leaked from Sherri's mouth and she clutched her chest. McKenzie spoke from the front seat: "she said she ate something."

"What?"

"She didn't want to get caught. So, she ate it. That's what she said."

"Christ." Candice's mind raced. This wasn't like any heroin OD she'd ever seen. It looked like a heart attack.

"Call dispatch. Move your ass. We need an ambulance," she barked as she dove out the door and rounded the car to the trunk. Rifling inside she grabbed their kit and the naloxone; her hands shook badly as she pried off the colored caps and assembled the tube. She raced to the backseat and climbed on top of convulsing Sherri, holding her chin to steady her face as she stuck the tube up her nose and pressed the plunger. She did the second nostril. She held her breath.

"What's supposed to happen?" McKenzie asked from behind her, Candice was startled, she'd forgotten he was there.

Sherri's face turned from scarlet to blue. Candice began CPR. "Not this," she said.

. . .

Candice took a deep breath and looked up. The investigator had his hand on his chin.

"Thank you, Ms. Nix. I'm sure that was hard for you. I'm sure you understand the pressure I'm under. That we are under as a department to figure out what went wrong here."

Candice didn't answer. She didn't care about the pressure that he was under. She'd read about the lawsuit from Sherri's family. She thought about the parade of children, damp cheeked and wide eyed. She hoped they won.

"So, I'm going to ask you again, the original question, the reason we're here. And I'm going to remind you, that you said earlier that you wanted Sherri to have justice, you wanted her family to know the truth. And, I believe you. So, I'm going to ask you, are you responsible for Sherri Thompson's death?"

If not for the camera, she would have screamed. She would have thrown the chair, beat her fists on the wall, fallen to her knees on the linoleum tile and made him feel as helpless and futile as she felt. As she was.

Of course, she held herself responsible. Couldn't he see? Wasn't he looking at her? Everything from her thinning hair to her wrinkled dress was an admission. Her failed marriage, the mountain of vodka bottles in the bottom of her garbage can, and her inability to sleep were all the evidence he needed. Candice's stomach rolled and she remembered the gleaming white bowl of the McDonald's toilet and she wondered for the thousandth time if maybe she'd spent longer in there than she'd had to. She wondered if she'd reminded McKenzie to keep his eyes on Sherri. She wondered if she should have realized when Sherri's face bloomed crimson that it was meth and not heroin that she'd eaten and that the naloxone Candice had administered was use-less. She wondered if any of this would have happened if she'd been sober. If this was even a job she was able to do sober.

"Candice?" The investigator prodded.

She looked him in the eye. His were blue and clear and the skin beneath them was smooth. She couldn't remember the last time her eyes looked like that. "I did everything I could, every-thing I knew to do."

Picking the Carcass

Janelle was sweating, sprawled on the threadbare couch, ticking fan pointed at her undercarriage, when the power died; the *click-click* of the blades coming slower and slower.

"Girls!" she hollered. "Girls!" Four and eight, they were sweaty too. The little one's hair frizzed into a white blonde halo. "Make sure the windows are open, and strip down to just your shirt and panties, okay? Maddie take your socks off, baby. It's over a hundred degrees. You don't need socks."

Maddie started explaining that she didn't like the damp feel of the carpet on her feet, but Janelle couldn't hear her over Rudy barking outside. "Christ, that goddamn mutt," she whispered, picked up an old bill for something, and fanned her face with it. The ear-splitting bark seemed even louder in the new silence. She could feel each howl in the hinge of her jaw.

The cut off wasn't a surprise. She knew she didn't pay the bill. She didn't pay any of the bills. To pay bills a body needed to have actual money, not SNAP, not an IOU, not a favor. Janelle rarely had any of them, but never any cash.

"I'm hungry, Mama," the baby said.

"You two go sit out back, sun's going down, it'll be cooler out there with the breeze. I'll find something." But when she looked in the fridge, there was only ketchup. *Food would have spoiled*

11

anyway, she thought, opening the freezer, stretching to the back, and pulling out the only thing in there: a box of old ice cream. No clean bowls, so she scooped it into three mugs with a soup spoon, and carried them to the backyard, wondering what horror she was going to have to do to get that power back on.

• • •

"Ice cream for dinner?" Maddie said.

"This will cool you off."

"What are the brown things?"

"Raisins."

"Why is mine crunchy?"

"It's just ice, baby. I'm sorry. I didn't buy the ice cream. Remember when Uncle Vernon came over and brought treats for you, and you watched a movie in your room?"

"When we couldn't come out?"

Janelle nodded. She hadn't remembered that part.

"Yeah," Maddie said. "He brought old man food."

Janelle didn't like rum raisin either and Vernon brought other weird snacks for the children, too: Funyuns and ginger ale. But it had been nice that he even thought of them, most didn't.

"What y'all doing back here," Jesse asked, walking around the side of the house.

"Daddy!" The girls screamed and ran to him.

"Power's out," Janelle said.

"You should pay your bills."

"You should pay *your* bills. You owe me three months."

"You owe me for summer camp."

"Bible camp? I thought it was free? I know you didn't come here for money. You know I don't got any."

"I thought you might be in the mood?" His eyes slid to the back door.

"Oh," she said and looked in the girls' mugs. She was and it was about the only thing he was any good for. She had a little time before it was fully dark. "I could be convinced." She rose, her spoon clicked against the side of her mug. "You girls stay here. I'll be right back. Don't leave the yard."

• • •

After, as Janelle pulled her panties up her damp legs, she said: "Leave me a bit for later?"

"I don't have more," Jesse said buckling his belt.

"You do. You always do."

"You're getting too skinny. You don't want your teeth to look like Misty's."

"I got a long time. I'll quit before then," she said, putting her hand on his chest. "If I quit you won't be able to come over here and get this whenever you want."

"It's getting dark. You better let those girls in."

"You can tell me how to raise those girls when you start paying for them. While I'm all on my own, I do what I fucking want."

Her chances for more fun later without him were gone, but she didn't want him to know she'd forgotten about the girls or that there was all sorts of shit back there that she didn't want them getting into: bales of barbed wire, a stupid deep ditch, woods that she heard all sorts of creepy shit coming from. Plus Barry, her landlord and neighbor, had warned her not to let her girls on his land or mess with his fancy horses. The last time she'd used the girls' safety as a lever to try to wedge some money out of Jesse he'd threatened to call Child Protective Services. Jesse was halfway out the front door when he said, "Oh, before, the dog was going fucking nuts. If he gets off that chain the county is going to catch him and kill him. And they'll send you the bill, too."

"Did you go see why?"

"Not my dog. I don't even know why you have it. There were some lights out in the field when I got here that's probably it, he's a dummy."

He said she got too crazy, too emotional when she was high, so she couldn't tell him that Rudy made her feel safe. It didn't make any sense. He was dangerous, a big pit mix, and she was afraid of her girls being around him. But she liked the look on bill collectors' faces when they pulled into the yard and saw him. In the night, no one could get anywhere near the house without Rudy letting her know. She didn't have anything of value, but that didn't mean someone wouldn't try to take it. A dead body was the easiest to rob, and she was near a corpse, just bones really, no meat left. She could hear Rudy barking when she called the girls back into the house, so after she got them through a cool shower and into their damp beds, she found a flashlight and went to see what his problem was.

Halfway, she stopped. His barks were frantic, goose flesh broke out on her arms. Something was wrong. *How long has he been like this?* Time always took on a liquid quality when she was getting spun out. She turned and went back to the house for the shotgun. Shining the beam of the flashlight on Rudy, he was at the end of his tether, furiously stretching towards the road where there was a dark lump. Roadkill, or trash thrown from the bed of a truck, likely. *Fucking dummy, nearly giving himself a stroke over garbage.* No strange lights, but Jesse was tweaking so he was probably seeing shit. She walked closer to the lump knowing that she was going to have to deal with it if she wanted Rudy to calm down, if she wanted to be able to get any sleep. "Please, please, please be a trash bag. Oh, or a backpack full of money."

But it was a raccoon in a puddle of something dark. She put the shotgun down on the side of the road and found two sticks. Janelle pinched the flashlight beneath her chin, and with a stick in each hand, slipped them under the thickest parts of the raccoon. She lifted gently, her hands shaking, and the animal fell off the sticks and back down into the puddle of its own goo. She felt something wet splatter against her bare legs.

She tried again.

And again.

Rudy was losing his ever-loving mind, and she couldn't hear herself think. Janelle finally grabbed the raccoon's tail, pulled it across the road, and pushed it into the ditch with her foot. As it rolled down the steep bank, the beam of her flashlight caught something shiny.

"Oh shit," she said and put her palm to her forehead trying to picture the animal she'd tried so hard not to look at. *It was a raccoon, wasn't it?* It'd been so mangled she couldn't be sure, and now that it was under some brush she couldn't really see. *What if it was someone's cat? And that glint was the tag on a collar reflecting?* She'd be devastated if Rudy disappeared. She climbed down the bank into the ditch and found the animal. No cat tag. No poor owner to call. Relief. But there was a metallic shine. *Fucking scavengers. They eat everything, it's probably a beer cap.* But still she squatted closer, curious now, and grabbed a stick and poked at the body. *It looks… no it can't be.* She tried to pry it out with a stick but it wouldn't budge. She stood and put her hands on her hips, chewed her lip. Then she squatted down, stuck her hand into the raccoon's remains, and wrapped her fingers around the lump. She pulled it out and looked at it under the beam of the flashlight.

A gold nugget.

What the fuck. Did gold still come in nuggets? Is that what they are called? Maybe knobs? No, nuggets, like chicken. Where do I even know about gold nuggets from? Bugs Bunny? Scrooge McDuck? Cartoons, right, this isn't real. Can't be real. Someone is fucking with me. This is some kind of joke. There is no way this raccoon is dead on the road with gold inside him. It must be something else. She looked around, swept the bushes with her flashlight looking for who was fucking with her. Looking for Jesse. But she couldn't imagine him touching a dead animal, let alone planting something in one. *If no one is fucking with me…* The lump was heavy in her palm. *Gold is heavy, right? How did you test if something was gold? Try to bite it?* She looked at it closely, black with blood and glinting in the beam of her flashlight. *I can't put it in my mouth…*

She rubbed it on her shirt and looked at it again. *Maybe just my teeth? Not my lips. If I can bite with just the edges of my teeth and my skin doesn't touch it.* She closed her hand around it. *Does it matter if it is gold? Yes. Bills. Food. My girls at home with no breakfast in the morning.* She bit down. It gave. *Was it supposed it give?* She couldn't remember if that meant that it was real or not. *But what if it is?*

Then she stuck her right hand back in to see if there were more.

• • •

She was exhausted and itchy, but Janelle felt really good walking out of the pawn shop with money in her pocket. She went to the gas station and paid her power bill, and then put fuel in her car. Then she went to Food Lion before she could make a stupid decision. She filled her cart and was checking out when the cashier pointed to the bottle of conditioner and said: "You can't use SNAP for that."

"I got cash," Janelle said and she enjoyed the scowl that wiped over that know-it-all's face. But then the money was gone. And she just had to be happy that she was picking up her girls from camp, not riding on fumes, and that she could take them home and put them in front of the window air conditioner while she cooked them dinner. It had to be enough.

"Mommy, Mommy," Maddie started as soon as they got in the car.

"Seat belts," Janelle said.

"Mommy, I want—"

"Is your seat belt on? I can't afford a ticket." When she heard two clicks she put the car in drive and pulled out of the church parking lot before anyone invited her to a service.

"Mommy! Nevaeh is having a birthday party and I'm invited and I want to go. Please! Everyone is going."

"Well now, I don't know baby, we don't really have anything to bring her for a present."

"It's not till the weekend and it's at the trampoline place! It's going to be so, so, so cool. And everyone is going, and I never get to go. And we don't *have* to bring a present."

Janelle rubbed her forehead with her hand. She remembered third grade. Hand-me-downs, never enough lunch, and never knowing if her mama was going to be at the bus stop when she got off. She remembered hearing about the parties. Never being asked to join. It was hard enough for the kids with no money to get invited in the first place, Maddie couldn't show up to a fancy party like that empty handed. "We'll see baby." She scratched at her arms. Just when she thought she was getting her shit together something else came to remind her that she was a bad mother.

She pulled into her driveway and turned off the car.

"No Rudy," the little one said.

"Oh shit," Janelle said. His rope stretched across the yard like a headless snake. "Go in the house," she hollered as she ran for the back fence and discovered the big hole. Barry was going to kill her. Not with his rifle, which he was known to carry, but with a big fat bill on pink paper taped to her front door. She prayed first that the dog would come home. Second that whatever damage he was inevitably causing couldn't be tied to him. *Just no evidence, baby.*

She went in the house and made the girls store brand mac and cheese for dinner. She smiled, *who'd have thought, with actual milk, not just margarine.* They watched *Dinosaur Train* and then she sent them to bed so that she could find Rudy before it was black. She grabbed the flashlight, and the shotgun, right away this time. She also licked the spoon and a little plate that she and Jesse had used the night before as a little present to herself for spending her money responsibly, but also because she was so beat she wasn't going to make it otherwise.

It didn't take long. He was a big dog, and she knew he'd go for the woods. He had found some treasure—his muzzle covered in gore—before someone found him with at least two bullets, from what she could see.

"Oh fuck. My sweet boy. Christ, I can't even take care of a dog."

She couldn't let scavengers eat him, but she couldn't carry him, so she grabbed his back legs to drag him deeper into the woods where she could hopefully pile some rocks on him. But damn it if she couldn't move him. "Fuck, Rudy. You fat beast." She yanked more but he wouldn't budge. She knelt down, emotion stealing all of her energy. "Damn it, I can't even bury my fucking dog." She petted his velvet head and rubbed his belly.

It was harder than she'd expected.

With lumps.

"What the hell?" she said, massaging his undercarriage. It definitely didn't feel right.

She remembered the raccoon. *I'm fucking high again though. That's all, I'm hallucinating.* She just needed to leave him, and call Jesse in the morning for help. He'd help her, if only because then she'd owe him. But then she'd pay him back and maybe he'd leave her a little treat. She found herself chewing on her lip and running her palms up and down her arms. But then she thought about that raccoon again, and how if there was gold in Rudy's belly, she didn't want Jesse to get any of that money. Jesse who always had gas for his car, clean clothes, and drugs, but never enough money to help feed his girls. She knew he was a regular down at Shifty's, too. She couldn't remember the last time she drank a beer in a bar. That money was hers.

She didn't have a way to cut Rudy open. She looked for a sharp rock. Nothing. She picked up the shotgun and held it against the skin of the dog's belly, whispered, "I'm so sorry, Big Guy," and pulled the trigger.

Droplets peppered her face, but she didn't care. It hadn't sounded right. It didn't sound like shooting an animal, like meat and blood. The shot sounded like metal on metal. She couldn't breathe. Back on her knees she was up to her elbows in Rudy's midsection. Her hands full of bloody golden nuggets shining in the moonlight. A flash of white light drew her attention to the trees. It bobbed between them. Someone had heard the shot. She wasn't sharing. And Barry had forbidden her from coming on his land. She'd lose her treasure and her house if he found her. She filled her pockets and grabbed her gun and flashlight but didn't turn it on as she ran for the fence.

"Sorry, Rudy," she whispered as she climbed through the tall grass, poke weed, and goldenrod, and back through the fence before she turned to see if she could still see the lights. The night was black. She pulled her hair out of her face and caught her breath. This wasn't real. No one found gold in their dog. No one like her found gold anywhere. If her pockets weren't so heavy, she might have thought she dreamed the whole thing.

• • •

As Janelle slid her handfuls of nuggets over the pawnshop counter, she noticed that one had a crust of dried blood, and she tried to pick it off with her thumbnail before the clerk noticed. She was almost finished when he asked: "Barry give these to ya?"

"What now?" she asked, trying to buy time. *How could she explain?*

"Barry is the only guy around here that has these, far as I know. Collects 'em. Kinda a weird thing to collect but he's nuts about them. I've been trying to get him into guns. At least guns you can use, and they hold their value. Maybe he's come to realize these are a tough investment. Maybe he's trying to get rid of 'em? Y'all are neighbors, ain'tcha? He give these to you?" His eyes were narrow and hard and didn't leave her face.

"Nah," she said, licking her lips. "I inherited them from my granddaddy. He was a miner."

"Well then. I bet Barry will want them."

"You gonna give me more than just their weight value then?"

"Nope." He piled them on a scale. "If you wanna take the risk and take them to Barry, you can. They're worth more to him than to me."

"I'd rather have the money now."

He looked at her again and she was sure that he could tell she was lying. Wasn't everyone trying to pawn something lying, though? Either to him, or to themselves? What did he care where they came from? She needed to feed her babies.

•••

Later at home, after she'd sat next to Rudy's water bucket and cried, she paid more bills and yet again had an empty wallet. While she was microwaving some hotdogs and warming some beans, she got to thinking about Barry's weird collection, how it got in those animals' bellies, and how she could get her hands on more of it. She was pouring Tampico into the little one's sippy cup when she heard the snap.

"Goddamn vermin," she said. Maybe if she could get a little more money she could get the girls out of this place. There was a nice new fourplex on the other side of town, she wondered what the rent was. Sure would be nice to be closer to town. Nice to be in a new place where the ceilings didn't sag, the floor didn't have mushy spots, and she didn't have to pray to get the toilet to flush or the sink to drain. And then she wondered about that mouse. She hurried to dish up the beans and wieners and got the girls settled in front of *Daniel Tiger*.

She opened the door to the cabinet beneath the sink, where she knew the mouse in the trap would be, and said a prayer it was already dead. She usually didn't check on 'em so quick, not wanting to find one in the throes, but she had to know. She held her breath as she pulled it out and set it on the counter. Its eyes were open, but it wasn't moving. It was fluffy, a brown and white field mouse that looked an awful lot like her fourth-grade class hamster. Its belly did look kinda distended though. Her heart beat faster. She prodded it with the tip of her index finger. It was too firm. Electricity ran down her arms. She opened the utensil drawer and looked for something sharp. She had a paring knife that would barely cut an apple, and a steak knife she'd stolen from a restaurant. Her stomach turned at the thought of having to saw.

She picked up the paring knife and pointed it at the animal's belly. Then she stopped and walked around the corner to check on the girls. Still TV zombies. She went back to her dissection, although it was feeling far grislier than anything she'd done in high school. She wished for the distance of that sharp formaldehyde smell, not this warm-fur pet scent. She closed her eyes, took a deep breath, and pressed the knife into the mouse until she hit the trap beneath it. She didn't feel anything hard like the nuggets, but it was difficult to tell. She spread open the cut. She still couldn't see. She couldn't imagine sticking her bare finger inside. Not here in the kitchen. Not sober. So, she used the side of the blade to put pressure on the animal's abdomen and try to squeeze something out.

When it popped out it startled her. But it wasn't a nugget. Janelle realized this mouse was almost a mama. "Aw shit. Sorry," she said. "I ain't saying you're better off, but you might be. It's tough out here for us."

Janelle put the mouse and the trap in a grocery bag and took it out to the garbage can. *I'm an idiot.* She wondered why she thought she would be so lucky again. Then she looked at the new stack of bills that had arrived that afternoon, *cause I gotta,* she thought. *I gotta.*

• • •

Janelle had just gotten the girls to bed when there was a knock at the front door. "Please not Barry," she whispered. She turned the handle and the shitty door swung loose.

"Word around town is you've had some good luck," Jesse said, and stepped past Janelle and into the house.

"You're hearing things."

"You ain't been paying all your bills? Paying cash at Food Lion?"

She snorted. "That's gossip? Shit, this town is boring."

"You gonna share?"

"Are you?"

"You know you're my girl. I'll always take care of you. But

I don't have anything right now. If you could spot me, I could get some."

"You've been hearing I'm paying my bills and you think I have anything left?"

"Shit," he said and stomped down her steps.

"Hey wait," she said running out into the grass barefoot to catch him. "You ever heard of anyone finding treasure inside an animal?"

"Inside? You mean like a prize buck? Or a bass contest or somethin'?"

"No, like actual gold, or jewels or something in an animal's belly. You know guys with a lot of money. Is that like a thing? A place to hide it maybe?"

"Shit, you're high as a kite aren't you. You used that money and got fucked up with someone else. I thought I was your guy, Janelle."

"I'm not, I swear. I'm straight. I haven't had any since you were here."

"No one fucking hides their treasure inside of an animal. How stupid would that be, if the animal ran off, your money would be gone." He pulled his hands through his hair and rubbed his face. "Speaking of gone, where's the mutt? He get loose?"

Tears started running down Janelle's face. She couldn't stop them. Before she knew it, she was on her knees in the dirt.

"You're crazy." He turned and disappeared into the night.

He's probably right, she thought.

• • •

Janelle lay in bed but her legs wouldn't be still. She couldn't stop thinking about Rudy. She got to thinking about how all the nugget animals were over at Barry's and how the guy at the pawn shop said that Barry collected them, and then she started thinking about the lights that she'd seen in his woods and how Jesse had claimed to see some over there the other night, too. She wondered if her story about her granddaddy wasn't that far off, if Barry was mining them. If there was gold in this ground. She imagined a little hole in the ground like a cave, maybe with a wagon that Barry pulled in and out. The she realized that all she knew about mining she'd learned from *Snow White and the Seven Dwarfs*. It might be harder than spotting a cave entrance to find Barry's mine. But all these animals were finding it, it couldn't be that hard. Finding Barry's mine and doing some of her own digging was way better than most anything else she'd had to do for money before. She didn't want to have to call Vernon or any of the others.

She slipped out of bed and put on a hoodie. She grabbed the paring knife from the kitchen, and at the back door she picked up the flashlight and shotgun. She had just slipped through the fence when she saw the lights in the distance and started heading that way. She was deep in thought about which bills she would pay first, or if she would maybe move the girls to that new apartment and wait for those bills to catch her again when she heard the scream of a coyote. She took a few more steps before she heard it again. Closer. And behind, maybe? She shivered. And then again, closer still. They were surrounding her. She racked her gun. The cries got louder and it seemed like they were everywhere, filling the darkness. She ran up to a grove of trees hoping to climb one to escape their imminent attack, and she nearly ran straight into the middle of their feeding frenzy.

A mass of moving fur was below her, writhing, the scent of flesh, of rot, solid in the air. They'd massed on something large and dead. *A deer. Or maybe a cow?* Sometimes when it had been a while since she partied with Jesse she saw things. Detox visions. She wondered if this was real.

She turned to leave and tripped over a branch. The fall knocked the wind out of her, and when she looked up, a coyote was only a foot away, mouth open. The wet of its tongue glistening in the moonlight. She didn't think, she just pulled the trigger. The beasts scattered. She took the knife out of her pocket and cut

23

the coyote open. She stuck her hand inside. *Bingo*. It was small, but it was there. She put the handful of hard objects in her bra.

Wiping her hand on her shirt and standing, she saw what the coyotes had been eating: a horse. A very expensive horse from the look of the parts that hadn't been savaged. She panned her flashlight over the poor beast, and saw the riding boot sticking out. "Oh fuck!" She ran to the boot and pulled it, finding it attached to a woman's leg.

"Are you okay? Hello?" she called.

"She's not," came a voice from the shadow of the trees.

Janelle pointed her flashlight at the voice: Barry.

"I really wish you weren't trespassing, that complicates things. I think I have you to thank, though, for recovering my collection. I didn't know it was out here until Billy called. I'd assumed she'd already sold it, and I'd lost it forever when I'd lost my temper."

Janelle didn't know who Billy was.

"Temper?"

"Well, you know," he said, waving at the mess. "I thought when Champ here fell on her, that was fortune shining on me. Nothing like a big horse carcass to hide a small woman while she rots. I was sad to shoot him, though, don't get me wrong."

"Billy, at the pawn shop?" she asked, trying to put the pieces together.

"Yes. Billy called and said that a woman in town, my neighbor in fact, had brought some new specimens and might I be interested in coming by to see. And, of course, I recognized them as mine and I knew the granddaddy story was hogwash, but I also knew that you must have found them out here somewhere, that she hadn't sold them before she tried to leave, that she'd taken them with her, probably planning to fund her escape. You can imagine I didn't want to go poking around in this mess. But time, and teeth, revealed what I'd been missing. I think I have your dog to thank for that, before I took care of him, too."

Rudy, she thought, and was filled with grief and rage. Then she thought of his belly, and Janelle looked down at the horse, she looked closely at its abdomen, it was littered with bloody nuggets, gore, and shreds of leather. "In its stomach. Like the rest."

"In the saddle bag, I imagine, perhaps her purse, it's hard to tell now. I didn't see them at first, but now with all the animal activity... they've gotten mixed with the remains, but also brought to light."

Janelle wasn't listening to Barry. *Just like the raccoon. Just like Rudy. The coyote, too.* It made sense, they were from this land, the mouse was empty because it was not. She wondered if all the animals on this land were full of gold.

"Champ was my best worker, I suppose he can be of use a little longer and hide one more body for me," he said raising his rifle.

But she was quicker because she'd already decided what she needed to do next.

She pulled the trigger and Barry hit the ground with a thud. She climbed on top of his legs and used the paring knife to slice open his belly. She reached inside as he screamed. There were only warm handfuls of soft. Her palms were black in the moonlight. She climbed off his body and turned back to the horse. Then she lay down in the grass and put her cheek on its nose. Velvet, like Rudy. Sobs shook her shoulders. She missed him so much. She'd do Vernon every week for a year if it meant she could rub Rudy's belly again. She closed her eyes and tried to forget. Tried to trick her mind like the drugs did.

The coyotes began screaming again. "Figures," she whispered against the horse's nose, "they're always circling. Watching. They don't even fucking wait until you're dead. Spend my whole fucking life just trying to keep them at bay."

She struggled to her feet, made a sling of her hoodie, and loaded as many nuggets as she could carry, each one a chance to put a little meat on her bones. They click-clicked against each other as she waddled across the field toward her babies, the cries of the scavengers as they descended on the bodies filling the night.

The Only Comfort

for Ryan

There are hundreds of things I should be doing right now, and not a single one of them is sitting on this deck, with snow up to my knees, and your sleeping bag draped over my shoulders. The sky, and the snow, and the lake, are all the same grey. Which is my favorite color, even though you say that it's a shade, not a color. You would roll your eyes, while I argue it can be both. I like that flexibility, of being allowed to be more than one thing. If you were here, you'd make a joke about flexibility and how bendy I am, even though we both know we'd settled into a missionary in the dark kind of pattern. But there's grace in flexibility, and we don't get a lot of that around here.

• • •

The fridge is full of weird food. You'd like it. Family sized casseroles. A whole cake and two pies. Maybe I'm allowed to get fat now that I'm alone. It's all rotting, but every time I go to dump it, I think about how twenty-five pounds of congealed lasagna is what my marriage is now. How when you slipped that ring on my finger ten years ago, and then pressed the back of my hand to your mouth, how I thought that was a promise.

• • •

Now, here I am eating week-old pie, straight from the pan, the filling separated, watery, and sour smelling. Wearing your sleeping bag over my pajamas that have become a second skin. Staring out across the grey, and thinking of all the things I wished I'd told you when I had the chance. That actually I loved your shower singing, and your morning breath, and how you could have cried in front of me.

, , ,

If you were here, you'd tell me to do something about the pile of cards, too. They arrive in the mail everyday like papercuts. Meaningless thoughts and prayers. I wonder how many times I popped a card in the mail, or ordered a delivery of flowers, when I should have gone over, held a hand, shared a shoulder. When I allowed myself all the distance from the reality of pain that money can buy. There are a ton of posts on my Facebook wall, and very few knocks on our door. I should write back and tell them if they really cared they'd come clean this shit out of the fridge, or maybe do the laundry.

• • •

I think I'm going to have to throw out my good coat. When the constable called, he told me to dress warm. We took the snow-machines out to the beach and they asked me if the things left behind were yours. I looked at the pile and told them yes, but you were obviously trying to lighten your load, for safety, for heaven's sakes. But then they showed me the phone they found in the snow. With the hundred missed calls from the hundred times I tried, and I threw up on myself.

• • •

We followed the trail onto the lake, and we saw how the tracks veered away from the safety of the white ice toward the grey. We got off our machines half way out because the ice was too weak to hold us riding. We walked out to a casket-sized spot where I could see the bubbles in the water below through the wafer-thin ice. I was just opening my mouth to tell them that these spots were everywhere in the north channel, all those currents moving fast around the islands, that it didn't mean anything, everyone knew that, when they unfurled your sleeping bag. I told them I couldn't be sure it was yours; doesn't everyone have that same Coleman bag around here?

"We found it right here," he said, and handed it to me and it smelled so strongly of you, even in the cold, even through my scarf, and the vomit crusted down the front of my coat.

"This could have fallen off the back of his sled," I said.

"This was on top of it," he said, pulling your helmet from the bag.

When I fell to my knees on the ice, the constable was kind enough to wait until I'd stopped gagging to tell me: "Looks to me like he ran into trouble over at the line. He went this way to get to land quicker. Engine died. He was trying to fix it. Looks to me like the ice just didn't hold out."

I didn't tell him what it looked like to me, that sleeping bag like a flag. Here. Here.

⦁ ⦁ ⦁

The phone is ringing inside. I pull your sleeping bag around my head and it still smells like you. Your naked body sweating in the heat of the campfire. Two weeks ago, I would have been horrified, today, it's all I can do to not put it in my mouth.

⦁ ⦁ ⦁

The ringing begins again, and it's not hope, but irritation that forces me out of the chair, and through the snow on numb, cement block feet. Inside, I reach for the receiver.

Immediately I can tell I've made a mistake. I hang up on the girl between car and warranty, but I've already seen the letter on the counter.

The letter that came the day after you didn't come home.

The one with my name in your handwriting on the front.

The one that I can't bring myself to open.

Of all the things I should be doing, I should read what you wrote me. Then I would know. But right now, it's an accident, and the pills that you didn't know I knew about, and all the injuries, and all the moods, are not anything more.

Right now, you didn't choose to leave me. You didn't break our promise. You were just in the wrong place at the wrong time.

So, I take the letter, and your lighter, and I go out to the deck and get in your sleeping bag, and I breathe deeply as I set the paper in the snow, and flick the stiff lighter until it catches, and I let the flame kiss your last words the way I wish I was touching you.

Buttons

illie didn't want to go play outside. She didn't want sunshine on her face, or to make mudpies. Meemaw wouldn't let her ride her bike down the dirt road to town, and Tillie couldn't imagine using the heavy yellow phone in the kitchen to call someone from school to come over and play, not with Meemaw's collection all over the house. She wanted to stay in, and read the new book she got at the library, and wait until Meemaw fell asleep in her chair, and then sneak some cookies from the jar real quiet. But Meemaw said Tillie was making too much racket for her to hear her stories, and besides young girls need fresh air to grow strong, she said. She also said Tillie should be seen and not heard, should keep her knees together, and that she should always wear a smile (even if she didn't feel it on the inside). Meemaw had a lot of opinions about how to raise young ladies, most of them had to do with Tillie not growing up to be like her mama, like somehow it was Mama's fault what became of her.

Tillie patted Buttons, who didn't move from his place on the couch, and rolled her eyes, but then remembered the new shoes Meemaw had bought her for the first day of school next week, and ran to the back door. "Wear your rubbers," Meemaw called. "Don't go getting those new ones all muddy and ruint."

Tillie sighed, and frowned, and looked at her old beat-up,

three sizes too large, boots. The only good part about going to a new school, and a new grade, was the new things. Mama didn't ever have a lot of money for new stuff, and Meemaw neither. Tillie was used to getting her clothes second hand, her cereal in a bag, and making do. But the first day of school meant new shoes, and new pink rubber erasers, and pencils that no one had chewed on yet, and it was a tiny high point in an otherwise shitty summer. But there was nothing to do in Meemaw's yard except go down to the creek. No swing. No neighbors. No sidewalk for hopscotch like at her old house. The stupid old boots would get stuck, but if she got mud on the new shoes, or stained them, she would get the switch. She'd just have to be careful in the boots. She petted Buttons, who didn't move from his basket by the shoes. The screen door smacked closed behind her. She stood on the back step with her hands in the pockets of her shorts, and wondered how long she'd need to be out here before Meemaw would fall asleep, and she could go back inside and read her book in peace.

The afternoon sun made the skin on her arms and neck tingle. She walked toward the shade down by the creek. She picked up a long stick along the way and decapitated some black-eyed susans. She squatted in the shallows and watched the clear water bubble by, she floated her stick and wondered how long it would take it to get to the next county. Maybe next time she'd bring a note in a sandwich bag, tie it to the stick and see if she could get a pen pal in Tennessee, or even Georgia. She picked some pretty stones and put them in her pocket. The water was ice cold, it was always freezing, coming down from the mountains. Meemaw told her about how they used to keep their milk cold by putting it in the creek, back when she was a girl. Tillie imagined walking out to the creek in her jammies with a bowl of cereal and laughed. She picked some daisies and pulled the petals out, throwing them into the air and running beneath. Pretending the petals were snow. Pretending they were rice at the end of a wedding, and she was the beautiful bride. Pretending they were the soft caresses on her cheek where her mother's long hair tickled Tillie's skin as she kissed her forehead. She wondered if her mother still had long hair, or had any hair at all. Meemaw said not to think about that kind of stuff, but it was hard not to.

A branch snapped on the far side of the creek and she looked up to see eyes on her. Her cheeks went hot. He had seen her acting like a baby with the petals.

"Take a picture, it'll last longer," she said. He walked closer to the creek. He was a lot bigger than her: red faced, and sweaty from the heat. She tried to lift her foot to run back to the house but the boot was stuck. She didn't want him to see her struggle, to know that she was trapped.

"I've never seen you here before," she said.

"I've seen you," he said. "And an old lady with a little black dog," he picked up a stick and walked to the edge of the water.

Goosebumps rose on her arms. She shifted her weight, rolled her ankle to free the boot. She didn't like that there was only six feet of air, and some thigh deep water between them. He was peeling the bark from the end of a stick. It looked sharp. He whipped it through the air like one of those long bendy swords. It made it squishing sound.

"What grade are you in?" she said. "I'm starting third next week."

"I'm starting fourth," he said.

"You're big for fourth."

"We move a lot," he said and sliced the air with the stick. He kept moving closer. Standing in the water up to his knees.

"You're going to hit me with that stick and I'mma be pissed."

"So move. No one is making you stand there."

Her boots wouldn't budge. She slipped her feet out of them and stepped back into the dirt, and then scrambled up the bank in her socks. He looked at the boots trapped in the muck and smiled. He crossed the river and slashed at her boots with the stick, a loud whack echoed as the wood met the rubber with all his preteen power behind it.

"You should let me hit you with this," he said, smiling.

"You're crazy!" she said stepping backwards to run, but tripping over a root and landing with an 'oof' on her belly. Her heart hammered. The air parted and re-parted above her in a whomp-whomp sound like a helicopter slowing as he beat it. She scrambled to get her feet beneath her and then ran behind a tree. He stood, five feet away, a foot taller and twice as heavy, slicing the branch through the air, but his eyes never left her face.

"You ever been switched? Spanked? I bet it feels like that. I'll do it across your butt so no one will see."

"I'll scream."

"You're no fun. No wonder you got no friends."

"I got plenty."

"I've been watching. I've seen everything."

Her face heated and her belly clenched as she wondered if he could see in the windows. "You weirdo. Who has no friends? Who has time to spy on girls?"

"I'm new. I haven't met anyone but you. But when I do meet people, I'm going to tell them what a baby you are. And maybe some of the other stuff I saw... "

"You're a jerk," she said, looking over her shoulder, gauging the distance to the house, and wondering if she could make it without feeling the sting of the stick slice across her shoulder blades or calves. She didn't hear him, he was fast and quiet, and she was on the ground again with the air pushed out of her chest and the boy sitting on her belly, before she could even scream.

"What if I just poke you," he said, pressing the sharp end of the stick into the soft flesh of her upper arm until it felt like her skin might just split. She didn't have the air to cry out, and she was glad. She didn't want to give him the pleasure.

He moved the stick to press into her belly just below her ribs. She only grunted. He moved then to the baby fat on her inner thigh and pushed hard. It burned and brought tears to her eyes. She felt the skin tearing. She imagined him drilling a hole through her leg, and pinning her to the dirt with the stick, before moving to her arms to do the same. Like one of those butterflies at the museum, trapped and spread wide open to for everyone to see, to touch. Prone and defenseless. "Okay," she whispered, choked.

"Okay!?" he was so shocked he tipped over. Finally, with his weight off of her belly, she could breathe

"I'll let you poke me."

"Wherever I want!" he was panting with excitement

"Wherever you want, if..."

"If what? What!"

"If I get to poke you first."

He thought about it. She thought she could see the gears of his brain moving. He looked down at his body and then at the stick, and then at her face, his eyes narrowed. "Deal," he said and stood holding the stick out to her.

Tillie stood slowly, brushed the grass from her shorts, wiped her hands on her shirt. A bruise was blooming on her leg and it hurt to let her thighs touch. She took the stick from him. It was warm where he'd been gripping it. She thought about running, but then about how fast and quiet he was. She thought about breaking the stick in half, but then he'd have even more sharp ends to torture her. She ground her teeth together, and thought about where she wouldn't want him to poke her. There was a long list, but she needed to pick the right one. The one that would stop all of this. She'd been watching his eyes, and she knew what he planned to do to her.

Then she knew.

"Come on, " he said, smiling, impatient to hurt her.

She struck fast.

He screamed like an animal and bent over double.

She knew she should be running back to the house, slamming and locking the door, but the noise coming out of his mouth froze her, she'd heard it before, through her open window in the hot night, it was the scream of a baby bunny being eaten by a cat.

"Shit!" he screamed. "You aren't allowed to go for the eye."

"You didn't say that."

"Everyone knows that."

She shrugged. "I didn't. Lemme see."

The eye was swollen shut. Blotchy, red and white skin with some purple starting at the corner. But she didn't see any blood and thought that was probably good. She'd moved so fast that she hadn't felt the stick enter his eyeball, it was all just soft and then hard, but when she'd pulled it out there had been resistance. She bit her lip. "You might want to get your mama to take you to the doctor."

"She's gonna whip me. We ain't got no money for that." He was crying now. Somehow that sound was worse than the bunny noise. "My daddy's gonna kill me."

Tillie chewed her lip, sighed. "Come with me, I can fix it."

"You can?"

"Yeah."

"Your daddy like a doctor or something?"

"You think I'd be living here if my daddy was a doctor? Shit."

"Your mama a nurse?"

Tillie had him by the upper arm and was pulling him back to Meemaw's house. "Just shut up. My meemaw is sleeping, you gotta be super quiet, and here, close your eyes, I'll lead you. It'll be easier on your hurt eye if they are both closed. Keep them closed."

She led him to the bathroom and sat him down on the toilet seat. She ran cold water over a washcloth, rung it out and held it to his face. "Hold this," she said, grabbing his hand. "Don't move. I need to go get a couple of things." She tip-toed past Buttons, to the junk drawer in the kitchen for the sewing kit, and supplies, and checked to see if Meemaw was still in her chair. Seeing her with her head tipped back, mouth open, and Buttons in her lap, Tillie snuck back to the bathroom and closed the door quietly behind her.

"Cookies?" he said, looking at the tin.

"What's wrong with you? When does this ever mean cookies?"

He shrugged. "I'm hungry."

"Move your hand, lemme see."

She had to use her fingers to push the flesh of his eyelid back to see the ball. He sucked air through his teeth. There was a dark gash to the left of his pupil and all of the white had turned bright red. It reminded her of when the birds pecked at Meemaw's tomatoes in the garden. Her stomach turned over and bile rose in her throat. She took a deep breath.

"It's just a scratch. I can fix it. Happens to Meemaw's dogs all the time."

"What? I'm not a dog!"

"Pugs. She loves them. Totally obsessed. They have these giant eyeballs, they get scratched all the time, so you put some ointment on it, and sew it shut for a day or two, and then it's fixed. You just gotta let the eye rest. If you keep moving it, it doesn't heal and they go blind."

"Blind!" he started to breathe quick and shallow, his shoulders jerking up and down. "I don't believe you."

"You can just go home."

"No..."

"She has, had, like ten of 'em. I know it's weird. But it's true."

He nodded.

She squeezed a line of ointment from the metal tube on to her finger, and rubbed it in his eye.

"Ah! Jesus Christ!"

"Shhhhhhhhhhh," she said right in his face, her spittle dusting his cheek.

"It hurts!"

"Sorry. I'm going to need you to hold still for this next part though. I don't want to jab you in the eye with a needle."

"Can't I just hold it closed?"

"No. It won't heal. That's what the vet said to Meemaw."

"But that's a dog."

Tillie rolled her eyes. "You're not going to forget, for even a second for the next two days? You wanna be blind?"

He sighed. "No, you're right."

"You gotta be quiet, too. We can't wake Meemaw or she's going to march us over to your mama, and you're gonna get switched."

He whimpered as she slid the needle into his lower lid, between his eye lashes and then the upper, and pulled it tight. Just like darning a sock, or putting a patch on her jeans. And again. And again. The skin came together in a seam, the black of the thread stark against his pale lashes. "Okay, she said, just one more thing." And she reached into the sewing kit and pulled out a round black button.

"What the heck?" he said, peeking through his good eye. "You're not sewing a button on me like a doll. That's probably just like a dog thing, to make the dog look more normal or something. We don't have to do it."

"It's important. Something to do with the pressure on the stitches. You don't want to rip these stitches, and I ain't that good at sewing. Besides, I got these sunglasses for you to wear. Start thinking about how you're going to hide this from your mama until we can take the stitches out."

He moaned a little as she attached the button, and then stood back to look at her handy work. The button was a little off center, and horrifying. It made her think of an old doll she'd found in a puddle at the grocery store once. "Perfect," she said. "Just like Buttons." She dusted off her hands and put them on her hips.

He sighed.

"Okay, now we just gotta get you outta here before Meemaw wakes up."

He whimpered a little.

She was so distracted by the relief she felt for having him almost out of the house that she forgot to tell him to close his good eye. When they got to the back porch, he was green.

"Which one of those dogs was Buttons?" He said, gesturing to the ten taxidermy pugs that filled Meemaw's house.

"They all are. That's the best part about pets. You never really lose them, when they die you can know what happened to them, you're not worried about where they are, or what they look like. They look cute forever."

"Was it their eyes, that killed 'em?" He says, pointing to his eye.

"Some of them," she said with a shrug.

"You're a crazy bitch."

"I thought you'd said you'd been watching me? I don't hide it."

He ran. She smiled until she went back inside and found Meemaw's eyes on her, Buttons still in her lap. "You can't treat boys like dogs, Tillie."

Tillie thought about the look on his face, the wild pleasure in his eyes as he pinned her down and pressed that stick into her thigh; the same look Daddy had the day he took Mama.

"Why not?" she said.

Sitting Ducks

"He said the building seemed secure but warned that if heavy rains fell, they could be dangerous for men on the lowest level. 'I can remember one flood to where the water came knee high,' he wrote. 'Those guys are going to drown if it rains enough.'"

—from *"South Carolina Did Not Evacuate Its Prisons for Hurricane Florence, and Those Inside Are Bracing for the Worst,"* **The New Yorker**, *September 14ᵗʰ, 2018*

Raindrops slapped against their ground level window. "I can't hear it yet, can you?" Amber said, lying flat in her bunk, but her eyes on the water flecked glass. "Jessie said it was going to turn and hit North of us at the last minute anyway."

"What does she know?" Glenna said from the bunk above. "Fucking idiot."

"She said North is good. It'll miss us, and swing back out to sea. Go fuck up like Africa or England or something."

"Don't you got babies up in Myrtle? You wishing this shit on them?"

Amber took a deep breath. She thought about her little ones at her mama's house. About their round cheeks and their big eyes. Her mama's half of a run-down duplex with its loose shingles, the single pane windows, the draft down the crumbling chimney; the car that rarely started, and never had enough gas to go anywhere, and the pile of bottles in the recycling. She didn't have anyone to call, neither of their daddies were worth anything, none of her so-called friends had it any better. She bit her lip and hoped her mama was sober enough to get them to the Baptist church, or the high school.

Something flashed past the window. Amber told herself it was a bird. Definitely not debris whipped by building winds.

"You won't hear anything down here anyway. Not until it's too late, then you'll hear all the water rushing down the hall. It'll be a fucking river."

"Water in the hall?"

"Don't you know nothing? Ms. Hot-shot high school diploma. Fuck all it's doing for you now. This whole place is below sea level, and we're in the basement. When the water comes we'll be like fish in an aquarium."

Amber sat up. Her eyes on the seal at the bottom of the door. "If it comes. It's gonna go North, Jessie says."

The rain splashed dirt up onto their window until they could no longer see out into the yard. Amber paced, her eyes alternating between the window and the bottom of the door. "Why ain't you scared?"

"I gotta plan," Glenna said.

Amber snorted. Of course, Glenna had a plan, she always did. Some stupid plan like having Amber distract Selma Banks at lunch while Glenna stole her pork chop, or having Amber risk her sweet job in the laundry to slip Glenna some extra socks. Lord knows what she needed those socks for. Glenna's plans always included a risk for someone else, for minimal gain.

"You know that secret phone of yours ain't gonna save you. You can't call fucking 9-1-1."

Glenna didn't even turn her head. "I can swim," she said.

Amber's heart sped as she looked from the window to the door, and thought about the one time she'd been in water over her head, a friend's birthday party at the Holiday Inn. The novelty, she'd never been in a hotel pool, and the cool green of the water, and the proximity of the solid concrete edge had tricked her, lulled her into believing when the other girls called her a chicken, and told her it would be fine to jump in, that it would be. She remembered the seconds of joy as she flew through the air, the crash of the bubbles fizzing their way up her body, but then how the chlorine burned her eyes when she opened them; when she discovered she couldn't breathe, that she'd somehow got lost on her way back up. How since she didn't know how to float, she'd sunk almost to the bottom, too buoyant to be able to push off, but too heavy to rise, to breathe, she was stuck in the limbo of the middle where she used up all her air watching the other girls swim above her, before everything went emerald green, and then black. Somebody's mom's boyfriend pulled her out and smacked her on the back until she could breathe again. She looked at Glenna and wondered if she would pull her out, or if Amber would watch Glenna swim by.

When the water level rose above the window outside, she closed her eyes and tried to remember how to pray. She knew how, at one point, as a child, when the thought of a big man in the sky watching her was comforting and not creepy, back before she knew what men could do, would do, if they had the chance to get her alone. It took prison for her to learn that women would do the same if they had the chance. Back before she knew that no one really cared about anyone else, that everyone was just out for themselves. Praying felt like asking for help and Amber didn't like doing that. It never ended well. Favors always came with strings and debts bigger than she could pay. Asking for help in school, she'd ended up on her knees behind the Principal's desk; asking for a place to live where her mama's boyfriend wouldn't hit her, she ended up with a black eye and a broken rib; asking for help feeding her kids ended up with her watching them pull out of her driveway in the back of a police car. She'd ended up inside, because to pay the never-ending list of fines and penalties she sold the last thing that she had, her body, only to find out she wasn't allowed to do that either.

• • •

A ripping sound, of seals stretching, of silicone breaking, of something strong finally giving way to something persistent, pulled Amber from her thoughts. She looked toward the sound and saw the paint beneath the window was glossy. She stood and reached her hand out to touch the line of shine that stretched to the floor. Wet. A trickle that she feared would soon be a river. Her stomach was filled with cement. The seal on the window was failing under the pressure of the water. She ran to the door and started banging. "Hey! Hey," she shouted.

No one came.

She pressed her ear to the door. The normally loud hallway was silent. She slapped the door, the flat of her palm cracking against the metal. "Helen!" she screamed, "Helen!"

"I can't believe you're thinking about tits right now," Glenna said.

"She's nice to me. She'll help us."

"She likes those blue eyes, and your soft hair. Probably thinking about what it would feel like on her giant thighs. Should I tell her I know?"

Even through the panic Amber could feel the heat rise to her face. "She's our best chance out of here."

Amber's feet were wet.

"Ain't nobody letting us out of here," Glenna said. "What, you think they're going to put us on a bus? A tin can of convicts stuck on 95 with all those minivans full of families and upright citizens? Can you imagine the television coverage? Nah, girl..."

Her hands still pressed against the metal, Amber thought about all of the locked doors between her body and outside; there were at least a dozen.

"Ain't nobody coming to save us," Glenna hissed into Amber's ear as she shoved her hands under Amber's sweatshirt and squeezed her breasts too hard.

Saving herself wasn't worth it, instead, she closed her eyes and grit her teeth, and begged the ceiling to keep her babies safe. "Please, please..." she whispered against the steel.

You Know What They Say About Karma

*B*rittney was about ready to jump out of her skin. She knew it was coming, the phone call that would change everything, fix everything, but she didn't know when. Her phone in the pocket of her scrubs felt like a timebomb. It was only her belief that this could fix everything, that kept her from feeling so damn guilty. The ends would justify the means.

She helped Mrs. Miller out of the bathroom and into bed. She tucked the blankets around the old woman's legs and fluffed the pillow behind her back. "Do you want me to put on a show?" she asked already knowing the answer. She picked up the remote and turned the channel to Matlock. Mrs. Miller's face transformed into a wide grin when Andy Griffith came on the screen.

"Oh, he looks just like my Lionel," she said. "Lionel was a bit slimmer maybe. But they both just have that goodness beaming out of them."

"That is rare," Brittney said tidying the room, collecting the trash and checking Mrs. Miller's glass of water. Brittney wondered if maybe Lionel had been the last of the good men. She certainly didn't know any. Or if maybe Mrs. Miller couldn't exactly be trusted to remember the details of a man who'd died more than a decade before. Bruises faded, after all.

43

"Can you just sit down with me a minute, Brittney? Take a break and enjoy a show." The old woman asked.

"Afraid not," Brittney said, not wanting to tell the woman that sitting and watching that awful show was not a break. That if she was going to take a break it was going to be out back with some quiet and a cigarette and maybe some candy crush on her phone. "I've got a lot to do before I can get out of here. And I can't be late or I'm going to lose my babysitter. She keeps threatening to raise my rates, too. Daycare already costs more than my rent."

"Anyone can babysit. Getch you a high school girl, or a Mexican. They work for cheap."

Brittney imagined it had been at least sixty years since Mrs. Miller had used a babysitter. "I like mine. I trust her and she's so good with Jamie. I don't know what I'd do if something ever happened to him. I'd just die. So, she's worth the money, it's just hard."

"You need a man Brittney, sugar. To take care of you, then you can stay home with that baby. He needs his mama."

"I like working. I just wish I wasn't the only one." Brittney felt her phone vibrate and her heart about near stopped. Her fingers itched. She couldn't check it here. She wasn't supposed to have it on her at work, but her boss knew she had a little guy and ignored the outline of it through Brittney's scrubs as long as she didn't ever see it in her hand. The phone vibrated again. And again. Brittney felt its urgency radiating through the fabric of her clothes and into her skin. *This was it.* She practiced saying, "I understand, Officer," in her mind. Practiced looking surprised. She'd raise her eyebrows, put her hand on her chest. She finished with Mrs. Miller as quickly as she could, hands shaking, mouth dry, and ran for the bathroom down the hall. She ripped the phone from her pocket and sighed when she saw that the missed calls were just from her best friend, and not the police.

"Hey girl," she said when Krista answered.

"You off?"

Krista was eating something. *God,* Brittney thought, *what I wouldn't do for some fries.* "Not yet, then I gotta get Jamie, and then go see what I can get for ten bucks at Ingles. Kyle is a bottomless pit."

"Speaking of Kyle…"

Brittney imagined handcuffs. She imagined Kyle laying on the ground, his cheek pressed to the pavement. Her stomach rolled. It was her fault. "Cops?" she said.

"No, why would there—"

"You see him with someone else?" Brittney said. "He's been acting so weird. And he never has any money. I don't know why the fuck I put up with any of it. I know he's using again. He's probably dealing, he's so lazy always looking for the easy way out. I wish I'd never let him come back." All the guilt she'd felt evaporated. He was a fucking loser and deserved everything that was coming to him. Fucking running around on her. Treating her place like a hotel and her like a maid.

"Calm down! I didn't see no other woman, but you said if I ever saw him doing something weird? Well, I was just at the intersection out at the highway, right there by Cookout and Chick-fil-A? And he flew through and ran the red. Craziness. So, I was thinking maybe he was using? That's not a smart light to run. Someone will clobber you."

Brittney pictured the intersection. Six lanes. Trucks from the highway. He had a death wish. "What the fuck. Probably trying to get to some girl's house, high off his face. Christ he's a loser, and I'm an idiot."

"Sorry lady. I know you hope that he'll figure his shit out for you and Jamie. But you know, tigers don't change their stripes and all that. Like you know, maybe let him go?"

Brittney wondered why she couldn't. He was no prize. He was only trouble. Why did she feel like she deserved that? *Why was she convinced if she did this the universe would be kind to her?*

"Oh, and why do y'all have that paint on all the back windows?"

"What?" Brittney said, hands going cold, a tingle sliding up the back of her neck. "What paint?"

"He doing some carpentry or something? There was bright red, red like lipstick or like a stop sign, all over the backseat windows. Like a can of spray paint exploded."

"Oh fuck." Brittney pressed end. She pressed the picture of Kyle's face on the screen. But it went to voicemail after the first ring.

Again. Again. Again voicemail.

She remembered the last thing he'd said to her that morning. "Oh fuck." She fell to the bathroom floor.

8:00am

The Home Depot parking lot felt a lot like gym class, Kyle thought, standing there like a jerk, waiting to get picked by the popular kid. He'd never gotten picked in school. Too skinny. Now though, skinny wasn't the problem. Kyle played with the lighter in his pocket and bit his lip. The sun was already hot on his neck and nose and he hadn't even started working yet. Soon, hopefully. He just needed one of these guys to choose him. Pick him, out of a group of idiots, standing outside hoping someone's crew was just one guy short today. He was the only white guy. It should mean that he's a shoo-in, cause they know for sure he speaks English, but everyone knows the Mexicans are cheaper and work themselves near to death. After two brown guys are picked up, Kyle lit a smoke and said "fuck it." He walked back to his car wondering how the hell he was supposed to stay on the straight and narrow if no one would hire him?

In his car he drummed a rhythm on the steering wheel and remembered that Travis owed him some money. Money wasn't as good as a job. A little now wasn't as good as the promise of more later, but it was something, so he drove to Travis's place, and pulled in the driveway. Travis' woman was sitting on the front porch smoking, watching a kid on a tricycle in the dirt where there should be grass. Kyle couldn't help but think about Brittney, about how she'd been at work for hours already. About how Jamie spends more time with the sitter than he does with his mama. How the sitter is so fucking expensive that Britt basically works just to pay her. He closed the door, and the woman on the steps flinched at the sound.

"Is Travis home?"

"He's working." She narrowed her eyes. "He owe you money? Cause he ain't got it."

"He's working ain't he?"

She pointed to the girl on the tricycle, "You got one of these? You got any money left over?" She stood and stomped out the butt. "Nevaeh, come here," she called. "Leave that and come inside." The little girl ran to her mama. "You should leave," she said to Kyle.

Kyle bit his lip and rubbed his brow with his hand, "You ain't got to be like that," he said.

She stood in the doorway holding the storm door open with her hip. "Sure do. You jobless bums always coming around. Trying to convince Travis that there is easier money. More money if only this, if only that, if only his family starves first. If only he sells our fucking bodies for the money to buy some nonsense that he has to sell to some other sketchy nobody. He always loses the money. No matter how big the dream. No matter how simple it seems. Easy money is a lie. The only way my daughter eats is if her daddy goes to work. She eats if he comes home with dirty hands smelling like sweat. That's what I know. Maybe, instead of coming over here and trying to collect some long-forgotten debt, you could, you know get a fucking job. Help your woman out, help your kid out, and get a fucking job." The screen door slammed behind her.

"Bitch," he said under his breath, shaking his head and climbing back in the car. He lit another and pulled out into the street. He wasn't a jobless bum. He wanted a job. Wanted to work. Maybe not enough to flip burgers, or bag groceries, but those were kid jobs, and no one in their right mind would expect him to do that. But maybe she had a point, maybe he could help more, maybe instead of finding some stupid job that only pays today he could watch Jamie so they don't have to pay for the sitter. *Fuck yeah*, he thought, *that's got to be saving like fifty bucks a day.* And Jamie is better off with him anyway. Maybe they could even do some jobs together, Kyle could show him how to build stuff. Then he remembered that Mario had his drill and saw. He should get them. He should probably pawn them. Britt would say he should definitely pawn them. Get cash. Pay a bill. But he'll show her. He'll fix some stuff around the apartment and maybe other people in the complex will hire him, and then he and Jamie could be handymen. It's a great plan.

He swung into Mario's and Mario was surprisingly happy to hand over the stuff, weirdly happy and even invited Kyle in for a beer. Kyle appreciated that someone wanted to celebrate his freedom. No one else seemed happy to see him.

Especially Brittney.

In jail, time moved so slowly it stopped, and he'd thought that maybe her life had paused, too. He'd held on too tight when she said she'd wait for him. He'd survived a lot of nights staring at the bunk above him and thinking about how excited she would be when he got out. How they would make a family together. How she'd want to take care of him and he'd never have to figure things out on his own. How they'd move forward together. But time hadn't stopped for Brittney or Jamie, and now Kyle was just perpetually two years behind, always trying to catch up, always in the way. Phones were different. TV was different. He didn't know where any of the right stores were and he was really tired of her rolling her eyes and telling him this or that went out of business over a year ago when he suggested they go to an old favorite burger place or drinking hole. He got it, he'd lost entire years, she didn't need to rub it in.

Mario packed Kyle's shit in an old duffel that Kyle was pretty sure Mario used in middle school, while Kyle drank his beer and watched another dude shoot at monsters in a video game.

"Sure you can't stay man? I'm expecting a delivery."

"Nah," Kyle said. "Gotta get my kid."

"Responsibilities man. Shit. Shoulda kept it wrapped." He handed Kyle the bag. "Thanks for letting me borrow your tools. Managed to fool a couple of guys into thinking I knew what I was doing. Enough to keep the lights on and the old lady off my back, anyway. Stuck something special in there for you for later as a thanks." Mario winked and bit his lower lip. Kyle wondered what kind of parole violation Mario had gifted him.

Back in the car, Kyle threw the duffel in the backseat and headed to the sitter's. If he did this Brittney would be furious. He'd have to show her how great this would be. When she got home from work she'd see how happy Jamie was, and how much money she could save, and then she'd get off his fucking back about getting a job. Maybe she'd even loosen up just enough to be a little bit fun again, occasionally. He thought about her smiling at him across a restaurant table, or reaching for his hand in a parking lot. He let himself entertain the idea that he might be able to start his own business. Be his own boss. How fucking awesome it would be to not have to answer to anyone. He pulled in the sitter's driveway, climbed the steps to the door and knocked. The sitter came to the door but didn't open it. Jamie was in her arms. She just looked at Kyle through the glass and shook her head. "You can't take him."

6:30am

Kyle was tangled in the sheets when Brittney closed the bedroom door. He looked peaceful like that, arms curled around the pillow, face smooth and relaxed. She knew he hadn't had a real rest in the two years he'd been in, always having to watch his back, sleep with one eye open and all that. She was glad he could relax now, maybe even heal now that he was out. Maybe he could go back to the guy he was before, the fun guy, the charming guy, maybe he'd even be better. Learn some responsibility. Get a work ethic. Maybe he'd actually help out. It was funny how all the things she'd thought were charming before Jamie arrived, like Kyle's spontaneity, or how he wouldn't think twice about spending his last dime on her, were the worst now that she needed him. She wished that he knew that she had slept with one eye open for the last two years, too. Single mom life. No one else to cook, or clean or get up with Jamie, unless like last night her mom took him. But that was really just cause her mom didn't trust Kyle. Never had. Probably never would. "Too much like your daddy," she said. Right before, "I thought you knew better."

The fridge was empty. She closed it and poured the end of the cornflakes into a bowl and wet them with water before scooping in a couple of spoonfuls of sugar. She'd have to go grocery shopping before dinner, but at least no food in the house meant that Kyle couldn't lay around in his boxers all day. He'd have to go do something or he'd starve.

Fuck, she felt so conflicted, but he needed to get his shit together. She knew the last couple of years had been awful, but it wasn't her fault that he'd gone to jail. He'd been out for months now, eating her food, using her hot water, leaving his shit everywhere and expecting her to clean up after him. She didn't need another kid. This wasn't what she envisioned all those nights alone, waiting. Something needed to give.

She scrounged a sort of lunch, a packet of peanut butter and cheese crackers, and a cup of applesauce, and tucked it in her purse. In the bathroom sink she sprayed some hairspray on her ponytail to try to control the wisps. Poor diet and stress were causing her hair to fall out. She didn't dare look too close at the purple bags under her eyes, or the where her scrubs pulled across her belly and thighs. Maybe it was better they had no food. She needed to stop getting bigger. She couldn't afford new scrubs. She turned out the lights and grabbed her purse and her keys and went out to her car. The sight of Kyle's turquoise monstrosity made her heart race. It was still parked illegally on the grass. She only got one spot at the apartment. Maybe he'd get towed. She climbed in and was about to turn the ignition when there was a knock on the window.

"Shit! You scared me," she said

"What time are you going to be home?" Kyle asked. He was shirtless, and she could see the train yard of pencil lead and liquid soap tattoos crisscrossing his abdomen.

Brittney did the math in her head. "Like five, why?" *Shit*, she thought. She should have said later, then maybe he'd be more helpful.

"That late?"

"Yeah. Got to get Jamie, and groceries. Unless you want to get some food? Breakfast stuff for Jamie, too?"

"I could get him."

"No."

"I'm his father." He put his hands on her door and leaned in.

That might work in prison, she thought, but all she saw were his soft spots, the places she could stab her keys.

"Who he doesn't remember? Who he doesn't know. You've been gone his whole life. You can't just barge in like that, it's not fair to him." *It's not fair to me either*, she said under her breath but he didn't hear. "He has a routine. Routine is important for kids it makes them feel safe."

"That's bullshit. He's safe with me."

"I didn't say he wasn't. I said the routine makes him feel safe. That's different. Fuck just give it time, okay? He loves his sitter. He's happy there."

"But I could—"

"I. Don't. Need. This. Right. Now!" she said, slapping the steering wheel. "I've got a whole day of work ahead of me, and I need to figure out how to get some food. Why don't you fix one of those problems? Instead of making new ones for me? Christ. Do some work. Get some money. Buy some food. I'm late," she said, raised the window, and put the car in reverse. As she drove out of the parking lot she watched Kyle in the rearview mirror, his arms crossed over his chest. He put on some muscle in prison. The first week he'd been home had been the hottest of her life. Two years of longing. Two years of fantasizing. The new hard planes of his body, the ache and fervor of time caused explosions between them. But then his ass found a home on her couch, and the food in her fridge disappeared, and worst, he questioned every decision she made, and disrupted all of the very carefully calibrated routines. He was unhappy, complained about everything. She couldn't do anything right. And then he started helping himself to her emergency cash, staying out at all hours, coming home smelling like mouthwash and gas station hand soap.

She knew what she had to do.

In the parking lot at work, she scrolled through the numbers on her phone. Pressed the one that said 'Kyle's P.O.' and waited. She was glad it was early. She was glad she could just leave a message. She didn't think she had it in her to answer any questions.

"Hi Barbara," she said after the tone. "This is Brittney, Kyle's, ugh, girlfriend, I guess. I think he needs to check in. I think he's using again and I think it's in his car." She hung up and felt sick to her stomach. She was betraying him. She knew. But it was for his own good. One little scare and he'd stop hanging out with his loser buddies. He'd get a job and start supporting his son. He just needed a little nudge, and maybe a night or two in jail.

11:46am

For sure the neighbors were watching. The yard was the size of a parking space, and he could see the yellowed lace curtains move. The houses were old. Single pane windows, that is if they weren't open to try to catch some breeze in this heat. Lord knew they didn't have AC, not here. Kyle stood on the porch, his palms flat on the glass of the babysitter's storm door, "why the hell not?" he shouted. He could see her throat move as she swallowed hard.

"It's not in my agreement with Brittney," she said.

"That's bullshit, you know who I am." He turned to his son

and he could see his big brown eyes were wide and growing wet. "Hey buddy you want to come home with Daddy?"

"That's not fair, Kyle he's three."

"It's not fair that you won't let me pick him up. You know that's bullshit. I know she's already paid you for today. I'm not asking you to give up the money. I'm just asking you to give me my son." Screaming shrilled from somewhere behind her.

"I have to go," she said and closed the interior door.

Kyle banged on the glass with sharp smacks. The inner door opened.

"You're going to break it."

"Just let me take my son home. Then you can deal with that." He pointed behind her. "I'm not leaving without Jamie. So..."

He watched her eyes slide back and forth between him, Jamie, and the screaming baby in the other room. He wondered how much he could push before the neighbor called the cops. He didn't figure he stood much of a chance winning the argument if the police got involved. Big tattooed felon versus babysitter wasn't much of a gamble. "You got to call Brittney," she said. "I'm not telling her and you got to call her before she comes here. If she shows up and doesn't know, I'm not going to sit for Jamie ever again." She stuck her head out the door and looked at his car. "You got a car seat in that mess?"

He shook his head.

"I regret this already," she said, opening the door wider so that he could step in.

The screams of the other child were so loud he could feel the vibration in his jaw. She passed Jamie to Kyle. "Here, just a sec," she disappeared around the corner.

"Hey big guy," Kyle said, "how you doing?" The boy's wide eyes blinked rapidly as they followed his babysitter out of the room. A building humming noise started coming from the boy and Kyle wondered if maybe he was holding a bomb.

"You can borrow this one," the sitter said, coming into the

room carrying a sparkly pink car seat. "I'll help you get it installed."

"I can do it," Kyle said, grabbing the seat as Jamie reached for his sitter. He knew if Jamie had a meltdown, she'd change her mind. He grabbed the car seat and ran out of the house. Only when he'd made it to his car did he turn and make sure she hadn't followed. He and Jamie were alone. He put the boy, and the car seat down in the gravel drive, and leaned against the side of the car. He opened the door and set the car seat in. He pushed against it with his palm and it wobbled and then tipped. That didn't seem right.

Kyle put the seat on the ground and then put Jamie in the car seat and clipped him in. Then he lifted the seat and the boy onto the bench seat. It was less wobbly. The extra weight helped. Then he took the belt from the back seat and strapped that over top of everything, holding both Jamie and the seat down. He wished he'd paid more attention when Brittney did it before. Jamie definitely wasn't comfortable. "Sorry buddy," he said climbing into the driver's seat. "It's just for a minute."

"I hungry," Jamie said.

Now that he had the kid Kyle wasn't sure what to do. He realized he'd never actually planned this far. He'd never thought she'd actually give Jamie over.

"I hungry," Jamie said, again.

"Okay buddy," Kyle said. "That we can fix. When I was a kid all I ever wanted was nuggets. You like nuggets?"

"Nuggets!" Jamie said, and clapped.

Kyle's heart beat fast in his chest, he told himself he could do this. He wasn't sure how to entertain the kid so, he turned the radio up and rolled down the windows. He sang along to the music. When they got to McDonald's there were three police cars in the parking lot. He swallowed hard. His hands were damp on the steering wheel. He killed the music. Jamie was sniffing.

"No like wind," Jamie said.

Kyle's eyes were on the police. He wasn't high. He wasn't

carrying. He was completely legal, and there was no reason for his heart to pound, or his palms to sweat like this. He pulled the car into a parking space on the opposite side of the lot and took a deep breath. This was fine. They'd go in, get food, no reason to be freaking out. The cops wouldn't hassle him with a kid. Still, he could still feel the burn in his wrist from the last time he'd had his arm twisted behind his back, and his front tooth was still sharp with the chip that had happened when they pushed him to the ground, cuffed and then kneeled on his back. He needed to get it together. He got out of the car and opened the rear door, tears were streaming down Jamie's face. Kyle was confused.

"Why are you crying?"

Jamie kept crying.

"Shit," he said under his breath, looking over his shoulder for the police. This type of helplessness was new and he didn't know how to deal with it. Anytime he felt trapped before, he did what his daddy did and hit someone. Distract from his own weakness by showing someone else who was boss. Kyle rested his hand on the top of the car remembering the Christmas his daddy had got them lost in a snowstorm, and how he'd punched the gas station attendant when he'd finally stopped for directions. In jail the social worker had called it generational violence. Talked about breaking the cycle. Kyle wanted that. Maybe the kid would have a chance if he grew up nothing like his old man. Kyle unbuckled all of the clips and waited for his son to climb out, but he didn't. Kyle squatted to get eye to eye with the boy. Jamie had his nose, and his eyebrows. "Buddy, it's okay. We're going to get nuggets, okay? You hungry? Is that why you're crying?"

"No like wind," Jamie said.

Kyle had no idea what Jamie was talking about, but decided that small kids seemed an awful lot like drunk girls. Super emotional. Borderline crazy. But food always helped with drunk girls, so maybe this would help Jamie, too. He carried the boy inside.

One happy meal, and one burger from the dollar menu courtesy of the grocery money Brittney gave him, and they were installed in a booth in a corner. The cops were on the other side of the restaurant. Kyle kept an eye on them. Jamie was too short to reach the table so Kyle set his food beside him on the bench. After Kyle ate his burger and half of Jamie's fries, he checked his phone. Nothing. It was funny, all while he was inside he dreamed about being left alone. Eating alone. Being able to decide by himself where to eat. Watching TV alone and being able to pick the channel. But now, he was always alone, none of his old buddies wanted to hang out, or if they did it was always to do something that would send him back to jail in the blink of an eye. Kyle guessed being alone all the time was better than having to share a shower with a bunch of dudes, but it wore on him; sucked at his optimism and threw shit on his dreams, but his handyman service idea had potential. He knew someone who could help, so he dialed, and was listening to it ring when Jamie tipped over his drink. "Shit," Kyle hollered and jumped up, grabbing the boy. Jamie's pants were just a little wet. They would dry. He switched sides of the booth. He couldn't see the cops as easily from this position but he didn't want wet pants.

The phone was still ringing back when Jamie said, "I got to go potty." Kyle slid out of the booth and pointed to the bathroom door. Jamie just looked at him, and then grabbed the front of his own pants.

"Oh no, no, no," Kyle said and then pulled the boy towards the bathroom and then into a stall with the phone trapped between his chin and his shoulder. That's when Jason answered the phone. Kyle left the boy in the stall to take the call. When he returned, still with no prospects after using the last of his dignity to beg his sister's ex-husband to help him find odd jobs, Jamie was still in the stall, pants down, pee everywhere.

"Well, shit," Kyle said.

"Shit," Jamie said.

Kyle rubbed his mouth to hide a smile. Brittney was going to be mad if she heard him say that, but Kyle couldn't pretend it wasn't cool that someone was actually listening to him. He scrubbed his face with the palms of his hands, tension ran in bands beneath his skin, his jaw felt like a vice.

"I guess we better get you home and into some clean clothes, huh?" Kyle pulled Jamie's pants back up, threw his son over his shoulder, and then leaving their lunch mess at the table, went straight out to the car. After another attempt at securing the tiny person, this time damp with urine, orange soda, and ketchup, Kyle was ready for a shower, and a nap on the couch in front of that British pig show, or the one with all the EMT dogs. But as they passed the park on the way to Brittney's apartment, Jamie screamed "slide!" at the top of his lungs, and didn't stop until Kyle pulled into the lot. When he put the kid on the ground, Jamie's pudgy little arms and legs started pumping, running across the mulch and up the ladder. Kyle thought it looked a little high, but Jamie'd obviously done it before, so Kyle went over to a bench to check his phone and to take a load off.

Jamie climbed all the way to the top without a fuss. Pride filled Kyle's chest. His tiny son was a brave little dude. As Jamie slid down, his hair flew back away from his beaming face, smile wide. He waved to his daddy. "See?" he squealed, and then ran back to the ladder. Kyle watched three more times, and then his asshole ex-brother-in-law called again and Kyle couldn't not answer, it could be money.

He felt the thud more than he heard it.

1:00am

Brittney rearranged the sheets around her abdomen, trying to hide her belly. Kyle couldn't sleep with the lights off anymore, so they were on, even though she would have preferred darkness. She wasn't in naked-in-daylight shape anymore. A baby, and years of struggling to make ends meet, made everything thick and saggy. She pressed her arms to her sides to push her boobs together. Maybe she could get his attention with a little more cleavage. She cleared her throat. Kyle put his phone down and tipped his head back, resting on the headboard. "I wish Jamie was here," he said.

"He'd be in bed now anyway," she said, blinking back tears.

"Still. You know, I thought I was going to get to see him tonight."

"You could have."

"I couldn't get here before you took him to your mom's. I tried."

She decided not to say something about how when one didn't have a job, or a kid to take care of, that there really was no good excuse for not being able to be somewhere by a particular time. He'd forgotten, or maybe he just didn't care, but he needed to make it her fault that he was a shit dad. "I just wanted us to have a nice night. Together. You and me. Relaxing."

"He's a really good kid," Kyle said. "He isn't a problem like other people's brats."

Brittney reached over to the nightstand, grabbed a big t-shirt, and pulled it over her head. She wasn't going to argue naked, "He's an angel. But even angels need dinner, and a bath, and a bedtime story, and a drink, and another story, and another drink, and then a monster check, don't forget the closet and under the bed, and then I would have to leave the bedroom door open, so…"

He just looked at her and she could not make her mouth say it.

His phone vibrated against the nightstand and he picked it up.

He had to be using, she thought, as she watched him stare at his phone and then type something. Lord knew he wasn't working. But she'd searched his stuff when he was in the shower and she didn't find anything. Prison had made him sneakier though, maybe there was something somewhere she wasn't looking.

His car, she thought, and nearly hit herself in the face. Of course. She was a fucking idiot; all this time it had been right in front of her. Of course, he wasn't going to bring shit in her apartment, not with Jamie there. That teal hunk of junk was probably a rolling pharmacy. *Although,* she thought, *surely he remembered she was holding for him, and had been for years.* He'd left a shoebox with all the shit he couldn't get caught with, but didn't want to lose, in the top of her closet. She thought about that box now, how it was just like her, closed away, waiting, unavailable to anyone else, but ultimately unwanted. She looked over at him but he was still looking at his phone.

Look at me, she screamed in her head. *Touch me. Want me. Why the fuck had she waited for him?* She could have had other guys. That one guy at work, who used to ask her to lunch all the time, and then her best friend's cousin had asked after her. She could have at least had dates. But she'd waited, stood by him, thought he was the one. Thought all that stood in the way of them being a family was prison, but now he was free. God, she was an idiot.

He put his phone down, and wiggled under the covers. She did too scooching close and pressing her ass to him, thinking maybe he'd get the hint and spoon her. He rolled over and faced the wall.

"Good night, then," she said.

"Night," he said.

Hot tears leaked down her face, soaking her pillow. Hours later he was snoring, she was still awake, playing the game where she calculated how much sleep she would get if she fell asleep right now. Two hours and seventeen minutes. And thinking about that box, and how he begged her to keep it, like he begged her to wait for him, and how all she ever had was his shit leftovers.

He could have them back.

She slid out of bed and pulled on a pair of his basketball shorts. Tiptoed over to his side of the bed and slipped his keys out of the pocket of his jeans, then carried a chair from the kitchen into the bedroom, silently, and found the box on the top shelf, at the back. Every time his snoring paused, she thought she was caught. She must have given herself five heart attacks thinking he was lying there watching. But as she put the chair back, and slipped outside into the night air she wondered if he even remembered the box. The box, her sacrifice, living in fear that the police were going to bust her with it. Or worse, one of his dealer buddies were going to come for it. Or even worse, that he had told a cellmate about it and someone he owed would break in and would stop at nothing, maybe even hurting her or Jamie to get it. She'd been living with an atomic bomb in her house and he didn't care at all.

The box was surprisingly heavy. She'd never opened it before. It wasn't just drugs. She suspected as much. She set it on the hood of the car and lifted the lid. Black metal gleamed at her. *Good*, she thought. That's at least two parole violations. Who knew what else he was hiding in his car. She unlocked the door and opened the rear passenger side seat, farthest from the driver. It was less likely he'd look over there. There was an old hoodie on the floor. She put the box under it, and then rearranged the fabric so that nothing showed. She thought about looking in the glove box, about looking under the seats, about smelling them to see if he was using, or if it was another woman, but realized it didn't matter. It didn't matter anymore.

When Brittney climbed back into bed with Kyle she couldn't sleep, but this time it wasn't anger.

1:35pm

When Kyle saw Jamie lying in a crumpled heap at the bottom of the ladder, silent, the world stopped. The playground ceased to exist. Kyle was in a long tunnel and Jamie was at the other end. In seconds, Kyle was on his knees beside the boy, afraid to touch him, but desperate to know. Moments felt like years, Kyle wanted to scream, to tear the grass from the dirt, but Jamie's chest eventually rose, he coughed, and opened his eyes. They filled with tears and he sobbed in Kyle's arms. Kyle had no idea how far Jamie'd fallen, no idea how badly he was hurt. Kyle looked around to see if there was another more parenty-parent that he could ask, but the only other parkgoers were playing basketball hundreds of feet away. Alone, like always.

"What hurts, buddy?"

Jamie cried harder. Kyle passed his palms gently over the boy's limbs, and they were all straight and functioning. His neck and head weren't bruised or swelling. "Come on, champ, you got it help me out. What's hurting?"

"Bum," Jamie said.

Kyle sighed, relief. "Can you stand? Walk?" He could tell the boy didn't want to, but it could be done. Kyle sighed again, and picked up his boy, but this time when he put him in the car, he knew he couldn't strap him into the torture device with the bruised ass. Kyle cleared the junk off the other seat and lay Jamie down. "There you go. Just lay down until we get home, okay? You don't have to be strapped in if you stay down."

Jamie nodded and put his thumb in his mouth. His eyes were big and his cheeks, pink. He looked like one of those ceramic children his granny kept in her china cabinet beside the liquor. Kyle got back in the driver's seat and started home. *Fuck, Britney was going to kill him.* His ice was so thin with her just breathing on it would break it, and here he'd taken Jamie away from the babysitter, who Brittney still had to pay, and he was bringing him home filthy and banged up. She was going to never forgive him, and worse she was never going to let him live it down. He looked in the rearview mirror, Jamie was sitting up, that was a good sign, but Kyle was going to get in shit if anyone saw.

"Lay down, buddy you got to lay down if you want to stay free."

Kyle wondered if maybe he should try to get her flowers, or do something? He had no money though.

Jamie was up again, digging around in the junk in the back-seat. "Bud, what did I tell you? Lay down, okay?"

Horns blared. Kyle wasn't paying attention to the road; he was watching the backseat. He tried to focus on staying between the yellow lines. *Maybe he could get her one of those cheap pizzas, have it warming in the oven when she got home, she couldn't be mad if there was pizza.*

An unmistakable click pulled his eyes to the backseat, "Jamie,

Jamie, put that down right now. Put it down!" Kyle screamed right before.

6:38pm (the day before)

On the ride over to her mama's, Jamie had fallen asleep in his seat. Brittney stood in the open rear door and watched his tiny lips move and wondered what his dreams were about. Puppies, or Peppa the Pig perhaps, she hoped. Something good, something that made him happy and not the types of things that filled her dreams: shooters walking into a daycare, or empty fridges, or watching her car get towed. She unclipped his belt and slid her arms beneath him, pulling him up on her hip and against her body, his head beneath her chin, his soft hair still sweet scented from last night's Mr. Bubble. The weight and heat of his body a comfort; it had just been the two of them for so long. For the millionth time in the last month she wondered if letting Kyle back into their lives was a mistake.

Her mama opened the screen door as they climbed the stairs, and ushered Brittney and Jamie into the house.

"You let him fall asleep in the car! Don't worry, I don't need to sleep tonight."

"Sorry, Mama. Just wake him up, chase him around the backyard a bit after dinner." Brittney said, laying him down on the couch, smoothing his hair back from his forehead.

"You know fifteen minutes in the car is like hours at night." Her mama had her hands on her hips. Brittney wanted to hide.

"I appreciate you taking him tonight. And for dropping him at the sitter tomorrow. I know you don't want to."

"I cherish every moment with my grandson."

"I know." Brittney said and cut her eyes at her mama. They both knew they'd both lay down in front of a train for the boy. It was Kyle that was the problem. Kyle was a wedge between them. It embarrassed Brittney, she wanted to be strong like her mama, but she didn't want to have to be.

"He got a job yet?" Mama said.

Brittney sighed and shook her head. She didn't want to start her evening this way.

"You look nice, anyway." Mama said.

Brittney looked down at her outfit. It was too tight. And everything she owned felt wore out. But she felt wore out, so she guessed that made sense.

"It's nice to see you with a little makeup on. If you wore it more often you wouldn't be stuck with Kyle."

"I'm not stuck with Kyle." Brittney looked at her baby asleep on her mama's couch. How could she tell her mama that she wanted more for Jamie than she'd had. That she wanted Jamie to have a daddy. To not worry about where his next meal was gonna come from, or who was going to pick him up from school, or if he was gonna have presents under the Christmas tree. Wasn't that what being a parent was? Putting herself second in order to put Jamie first? She bent over and kissed him on the cheek, "love you baby man," she said. "Love you, Mama," as she walked out the door.

"Don't get hurt," Mama said.

1:54pm

Kyle had watched his father beat his mother unconscious. He'd witnessed men stabbed and raped in prison. He'd seen an old woman piss herself as he held her at gunpoint and demanded what was in her till, but he had never heard a gun fire in a car before. It was impossibly loud. Ear drum exploding. Mind shattering. The kind of loud that filled every crack, every crevice with hot white. The silence after was a vacuum. A void. Nothing. He wanted his body to move but he couldn't figure out how to make that happen. First a blink. Then an-excruciating-nother. Then he could feel his hands tingling on the steering wheel, and remembered where he was, what he was doing in the before. Because now there was only before and after. Before he turned around, and after he saw what a bullet could do to a child's face. His child's face.

11:59 pm

Brittney sat criss-cross-applesauce on Jamie's bed, hugging his pillow. His closet door hung crooked, it had come off the track months ago. She'd been meaning to fix it. Now it didn't matter.

She couldn't stop thinking about Kyle in the backseat of that cruiser. The whole world had been cobalt. Everything she could see had pulsed blue as the lights from the cop cars washed over her hands, her mama's face, Kyle's shit box car covered in yellow tape, a stretcher with a black tarp over it, and the back of Kyle's head through the rear window of a police cruiser. She had wanted them to let him out, because she had wanted to kill him. Her skin was hot with rage as she imagined breaking the glass of the window with her elbow and pulling him out by his hair. She imagined kicking him until there was no resistance, until he was just a bag of bruised meat on the ground.

He shouldn't have even had Jamie.

He shouldn't have been driving him anywhere.

Why the fuck wasn't her baby in a car seat?

On the side of the road, everything crawling with people in uniforms, her mama had squeezed her shoulders. Britney shrugged her off. She couldn't stand to be touched. Didn't want to be comforted. When the coroner's office rolled the stretcher away, "Let's go home," Mama said. Brittney hadn't wanted to. Hadn't wanted to leave Jamie, that was what had caused this mess, wasn't it? Her leaving him. She'd have never let Kyle have him. She'd never have put that box in his car if she thought there was a chance. But when she could no longer heard the rumble of the stretcher's wheels on the pavement, or the squeak of its legs collapsing, there didn't seem much of a point standing on the side of the road rubbing her toes in the gravel, or fending off strangers trying to hand her shitty coffee. They weren't going to let her kill Kyle, and Jamie wasn't coming back.

Mama had wanted to go to her house, said it would be better, but Brittney had refused to get into the car until she'd agreed to bring her here. Brittney needed to be surrounded by Jamie's stuff, by his smells.

"If you're gonna be in here there's no use me sleeping on the couch," Mama said. "I'mma use your bed." She was standing in the doorway, Brittney's skin prickled at the thought of anyone else being in Jamie's room, changing something, ruining something. Maybe Mama could tell that, cause her voice softened and she didn't move to come in. "There's room for two though, if you want."

Brittney just nodded. She didn't want to sleep in there. She'd been in that bed with Kyle just last night. Before.

"I'm not going to say I told you so—"

"Fucking already? It's been what, a whole ten hours?"

"—but you know better. Kyle didn't. He is stupid like your daddy. It was only a matter of time before he did something like this." Mama crossed her arms in front of her chest.

Brittney remembered how Kyle had pulled his hands through his buzzcut and waved his arms around while he was talking to the cops. She had been too far to hear what the police were asking, but Kyle had been yelling. "He says he didn't know the gun was in the car," she said.

"Men and their fucking guns. He didn't know! That's rich. They treat them like toys. Did you know there ain't been a shooting in this county in the last two years that the state hasn't had to intervene in because someone involved is connected to the sheriff's department? That's how bad it is. Even the guys we pay to protect us are waving their guns around like cowboys, or they can't be bothered to lock them up." Mama slapped the palm of her hand on the cheap door and the sound cracked through the quiet of the room. "They should just use the guns on themselves," she whispered. "Save us the trouble. That's what I'd do if I killed my baby. That's what they deserve, karma and all that."

Brittney's eyes welled and her chest went tight. *Yes,* she thought, *that would be fair.* She could always count on her mama for the truth no one else wanted to tell. Baby killers deserved to die.

"Until this one…" Brittney cleared her throat..

"What now?"

"There's no police involved in this one."

"Well, we don't know that. Kyle says he doesn't know how the gun got in the car."

"He knows."

"No, you said—"

"I said he didn't know it was there. But he knows how it got there."

"How do you know that?"

Kyle had been a clown talking to the police, all big arm gestures and loud denials punctuated by sobs and mucus running down his chin. Until they showed him the weapon. He must not have seen it when it happened. Brittney imagined that he had been much more concerned with her baby than the gun. She loved Kyle for that. But when they held the plastic bag in front of his face his mouth had opened and not closed. His head had turned, looking for her, and when their eyes met his were wide and unbelieving. "I could see it on his face," Brittney said. Mama blew air through her lips and made a farting sound that would have cracked Jamie up. Brittney swallowed hard; she couldn't deal with any more of this. Any more and she would spill her guts just to put her mother in her place. It was Kyle's fault. Brittney had to believe that to survive. She needed to build a wall of Kyle's guilt around herself. The police believed it. She had to keep letting her mother believe it. "Go to bed Mama. Tomorrow will be long."

Her mother turned the lights off in Jamie's room as she left. Brittney sat in the dark for a moment, then stood, crossed the room and flipped the switch back up. She didn't deserve darkness. She went to the bathroom and peed. She washed her hands. Jamie's Elmo toothbrush was in a cup by the sink. It was dry. It wouldn't be wet again. She carried it back to his room and put it on his dresser next to clothes that he'd never wear again. She laid down in his bed that he'd never sleep in again, and got under his blanket that he'd never use again, and put her head on his pillow that soon would smell like her and not him, and realized that she deserved this.

Kittens

*C*heryl stood over the grocery store cooler; the fluorescent lights reflected off the plastic wrapped meat. She had ten miraculous dollars left in the grocery budget and after endless ground beef casseroles Tim deserved a steak. She ran her index finger over a line of white fat through the tight cellophane as her phone chirped and vibrated in her other hand.

This call wasn't a surprise; she'd been waiting for it for five years.

"Hello," she said after the third ring. "Yes, this is she." The voice on the other end of the line told her what she was expecting to hear. She wished she could say feared, but resignation had replaced fear months ago. "Thank you," she said, disconnecting and pressing the speed dial for Tim.

"Hey, baby," he said, seconds before she got his voicemail.

"I need you to pick up the kids from school and take them to my parents."

"Okay?" he said.

She could see his brows coming together in her mind's eye. "I'm at the grocery store, and then I need you to meet me at the ER."

He blew out a sigh. Static crackled in her ear.

"You left her alone?" he said.

* * *

The first time she'd gotten the call, despite the heat of the day, Cheryl's body felt encased in ice. She thought she'd freeze to death, hypothermia taking her on the ride to the hospital. Each subsequent time, she'd felt it less. Today, she was hot.

The first call, a lifetime ago, Hannah had been thirteen, and they'd made a thousand excuses. Hannah was naive. She was just a kid. She was confused or had been pressured, or didn't really know what she was doing. The second time, at fourteen, Cheryl was suspicious they were wrong. At fifteen, they'd made the flying trip to the ER three times, and found her themselves a fourth. Tim had stumbled upon Hannah and a friend, prone and blue lipped in her bedroom. At sixteen, Cheryl and Tim spent half their life savings on rehab and still found themselves in the ER twice and the county jail two more times. At seventeen, they spent the other half of their savings, plus some, on promises that she would change. But the only good that came from their bank account going into the red was knowing that they wouldn't be getting any emergency calls for a few precious weeks.

The emergency room waiting area felt like home. Her bum knew the seat. She no longer heard the slide and screech of the door. Memories of teaching Jack long division under the hum of the florescent lights; of watching Annie text her crush, her legs dangling over the side of the plastic chair; of reading to Ben from the ratty book he found in the filthy children's corner filled her mind. All of her children shallowly distracted, their worry for their sister, for their lives as they knew them, hovering just under the surface.

"Have you heard anything?" Tim asked from behind. She hadn't seen him come in.

"Not yet."

He sat down beside her, resting his elbows on his knees. She studied the thinning patch on the back of his head, the crease across his neck, the way his shirt clung to his shoulder blades. Holding on to hope had turned her hair white, and rimmed her mouth in tiny lines; it had stolen the hair on Tim's head. Cheryl couldn't remember the last time she saw him naked. They hadn't always been like this. Waiting to save Hannah was killing them.

"Were the kids okay at my parents?" she asked, curious but also wanting to break the silence.

"They knew why they were there."

"Well, of course." Cheryl closed her eyes so he wouldn't see her roll them.

"But yes, Ben especially was excited about the kittens."

"Oh shit, I forgot about the kittens."

"Yeah."

Cheryl rubbed her temples. Non-skid shoes squeaked toward them. She looked up and into the earnest eyes of a middle-aged doctor, the corners of his mouth turned down. His hands were clasped in front of his abdomen.

"Mr. and Mrs. Davis?" His eyebrows went up.

She nodded.

"Can you please come with me?"

• • •

It's not like they ever had a lot of money. They'd lived paycheck to paycheck with a hundred or so to spare. "Just in case" money they'd called it. In case she forgot to pay a bill, in case something small broke, in case of a field trip or group gift they couldn't wiggle out of.

Oxy and heroin were expensive. Not the drugs themselves, as Cheryl had recently discovered, they weren't a high-class high. But the fallout of addiction was financially devastating. Cheryl could still remember the first time Hannah went to rehab, the feeling in the pit of her stomach when she checked the bank balance before she went grocery shopping to discover she had to feed the family for a week on twenty-three dollars.

The kids were amazing. They didn't once ask for fancy shoes, or the sparkly new toy advertised during Saturday morning cartoons. Yet Cheryl lived in fear of birthday party invitations, school fundraisers, and car problems. She felt like a bitch for being so focused on money. It wasn't like her. She was a generous person, but it wasn't just dollars the drugs were stealing from their family. It was the way that Jack's foot tapped under the kitchen table, how his lips were always chapped, and his test grades plummeted when Hannah missed family dinner. The way Ben liked to make a fort behind the curtain in the front window—the coldest place in the whole house, but with the best view of the driveway. Annie stopped eating. Cheryl would take treats to her at midnight when everyone else was sleeping, hoping to tempt her shrinking daughter and put some meat back on her bones. Her heart broke when she would find Annie curled up in her sister's empty bed.

. . .

"I'm so sorry," the doctor said after they'd sat and the broad expanse of his desk was between them. Cheryl looked down at her hands and traced her rough cuticles with the side of her thumb.

"I'm going to leave you alone to process this. If there is anything you need, please let me or my staff know." He left the room and took the air with him.

Tim stood and paced, and ran his hands through his hair. Dark rings emerged from beneath his arms when he raised them. He finally stopped, facing away from her, studying the doctor's diploma.

"What do we do now?" His voice was quiet and low.

"Well, I'm sure there is paperwork, and I have a car full of groceries, and we need to get the kids—"

"No, I meant," Tim turned and shook his head. "Wait, what? You checked out at the grocery store? You got the call and then you waited in line?"

"I didn't have anything frozen, and we need to eat."

"She's our daughter."

"I pushed her out of my body."

"Oh, so this is how this is going to go? Who loves her more? Who is hurting more?"

"Not at all. I was going to say I remember exactly the moment she became mine. She was still inside my belly. It was the middle of the night. I don't know why I did, but I started singing. Ha! You know me, I don't sing. But I did then. You are my sunshine. And she kicked. It was the first time she had. It was the first time that it hit me that a person was in there. A person who was mine. I couldn't sleep that night with the weight of that responsibility resting on me."

Cheryl didn't know when she'd started crying, but water was dripping from her face. She used her sleeve to wipe it.

"I remember too the moment that she slipped away. Last year. She'd been home from rehab for two months. I took her to get our nails done to celebrate sixty days of her being sober. I was bursting with pride. This was the time she was going to beat it. I was a good mother. Everything was going to be okay.

"Do you remember? We thought she was actually holding down a job? We had conversations! She helped around the house! Two good months tricked me into believing. Then she got up from the manicure chair to wash her hands before they put the polish on. I was gushing to the nail lady about my brave daughter and all my dreams for her when Hannah's jacket on the back of her chair made a strange beep that I'd never heard before. I reached into the pocket and pulled out her phone. The screen was full of notifications from a messaging program I'd never heard of. I opened it. I couldn't believe it as I scrolled through screen after screen of messages. We weren't stupid. We'd been monitoring her phone, watching the bill. When she told us, she wasn't in contact with her old friends, we believed her. But we'd been duped. She wasn't sober; she was just better at hiding. She was a liar. All the money and hope we'd spent on rehab had just taught her how to trick us."

"Why didn't you tell me?" Tim's arms were crossed tightly across his chest.

"When she came back to her seat and saw me with her phone, she just shrugged, picked up her jacket and phone and left. We didn't see her for a week. I couldn't stand to tell you."

"Why?"

"Because we'd been so hopeful, and because it was my fault she was gone."

"It wasn't." He sat beside her and pulled her into his arms. It was the first time they'd touched in more than a week. Cheryl felt her skin suck him up like a sponge.

"I know that now. I know that she made the decision. But for the longest time I blamed myself that I couldn't fix her."

"You can't fix her."

"I know." She laid her head on his shoulder. She breathed deep the scent of the detergent she used to wash her family's clothes. He put his hands on her arms and pushed her away until he could look into her eyes.

"You're not surprised this happened."

"Are you?" she asked.

He studied her face.

She crossed her arms in front of her chest. "It was only a matter of time," she whispered.

• • •

Cheryl finished the paperwork while Tim picked up the kids from the farm. When she finally got home, she could barely move her shoulders for the knots of tension in her neck. She left the groceries on the counter. Tim sat in the dark family room, she could see the glow of the TV and hear the clink of ice cubes in his whiskey glass. She was sure it wasn't his first, but it was promising that he was still using a glass.

She mounted the stairs, feeling guilty that she didn't want to check in on the kids. Guilty in her relief. Shouldn't this be the worst day of her life? She didn't want to see the hope in their eyes or answer their unspoken questions. They had agreed breakfast was the best time to tell the children. Let everyone get some sleep. Maybe it wouldn't be as terrible a conversation to have in the morning. She craved a deep bath, for hot water stinging her skin to her chin and the random slurp of the overflow drain. Jack and Annie's doors were closed, but Ben's was always open. He was afraid of the dark. She crept by and heard only silence. She smiled as she pushed her bedroom door open. She wasn't a bad mom to wish for some alone time.

She kicked her shoes off into the bottom of the closet.

"Mama?" a small voice called from her bed. In the light from the hall, she saw there was a tiny lump right below her pillow.

"Benny! Why aren't you in bed?"

"I can't sleep, so I was waiting for you. Where were you?"

"It's too late, baby. We'll talk about it in the morning." She scooped him into her arms and carried him to his bed.

"What happened to the littlest kitten?"

She'd known this conversation was coming. She might be able to make him wait 'til tomorrow to hear about Hannah, but Ben wasn't going to let her off the hook about the damn kittens.

"Well, Benny," she took a deep breath. How was she supposed to explain the facts of life to a six-year-old, when she barely understood them herself? "Sometimes, in a litter of kittens, there is one that isn't strong enough and the mama kitty abandons it, and we have to take that kitten away so the others can thrive. You see, if that one is sick and can't make it, it's better for the others if it goes away."

"Where does it go?"

Cheryl was sure that her stomach was on the floor somewhere. It had fallen so fast and violently. "Don't worry about that. Papa took care of it."

"Is it always the littlest one that is the weakest?"

"Oh no, sweetheart. You never know which one it's going to be when they are born. As they get older you can just tell because that one needs more help, more food, more attention, and still can't do what the others can. It will never be able to take care of itself."

"Why doesn't the mommy just give the kitten more food?"

Cheryl was glad it was dark in the room. He couldn't see her face. Couldn't see the tears streaming down her cheeks. "She does. She gives that baby everything she can. Even taking food away from the stronger kittens, but soon she realizes that if she keeps doing that, they will all die. To protect the whole litter, she has to let go of one, or risk losing them all. But you don't have to worry about it, okay, kiddo? The rest are going to grow big and chubby and strong, and maybe we can go back to the farm and play with them tomorrow. Okay? Sweet dreams, little love."

Cheryl kissed Ben on the forehead and pulled his covers up to his chin. She walked to the door and blew him a kiss.

"Mama?"

"Yes, baby?" she answered, although she had nothing left.

"Is Mittens going to be mad at Papa? Won't she miss her baby?"

"With her whole body. For the rest of her life. But Mittens knew, sweetheart, she knew what needed to be done, that's why she left that kitten alone." She turned and walked down the hall.

Asylum

*L*ourdes muscled the cart over the cracked and uneven pavement of the Mountaineer Inn's parking lot. A spray bottle tipped off the side and burst when it hit the ground, leaking green over her shoe. The cart wheel was broken and had been since before she could remember. Dwayne, her boss, refused to do any repairs more substantial than duct tape or WD 40. He didn't care that at the end of her shift, all five feet of her hurt. At least, she thought, it kept her mind off the ghosts.

Dwayne considered himself a very smart man and liked to explain costs to Lourdes as percentages of their room rates, "Five nights! Five nights!" he'd shout across his scratched metal desk, and then laugh to himself, assuming her silence was agreement, or ignorance. If only, like her, he'd taken some economics classes, he'd know that keeping the cart was costing much more: the dwindling number of rooms that she was able to clean during her shift; the increasing theft of supplies as she was forced to leave the cart further and further from each room.

Instead, he screamed at her for being lazy.

He screamed at her for stealing supplies.

But it wasn't anything that she hadn't heard before, "thought your people were supposed to be hard working and good natured," he'd say, like he knew who her people were.

She pushed the cart harder, wrestled it into the storage room, and bent over to catch her breath. Lourdes practiced conjugating English verbs to keep from letting her mind wander. She studied English to help her get ahead, and because it was marginally better to hear "you're so articulate" than "speak English," from an angry man in a red hat, but also because it was numbing. The exercises and memorization kept her thoughts just busy enough to keep her out of trouble. Most days.

The door flew open and smacked her in the shoulder.

"Six wants more towels," Dwayne said.

"More towels? Now?" She didn't need to look at her watch to know she should already be at home. Lourdes sighed, put some towels under her arm, and left Dwayne rocking from his toes to his heels with his hands on his hips in her wake. On the way to room six she whispered, "I am. You are. He is. She is. They are."

She knocked on the door.

Nothing.

She knocked again.

Nothing.

This was not uncommon. Often people would call the front desk and request things and then immediately leave. Or get in the shower. Or go to sleep with ear plugs in. Lourdes preferred to think that these people were just forgetful or distracted. She'd been stupid and thoughtless before. But when these same people left her blood-stained linen, or shit in the tub, or a toilet clogged with condoms, or vomit anywhere/everywhere, she saw them for what they really were: assholes.

On the third knock the door swung open and a clean cut, middle aged white man apologized. A baby was crying in the background, goosebumps rose on her skin and a pain pinched the bridge of Lourdes' nose. They stood for a moment looking at each other. "Baby crying?" she said.

"No, there's no baby in here," he said shaking his head. And they stood looking at each other until eventually he said, "thank you," and took the towels from her arms. She didn't move. She couldn't move. "Oh," he said to her just standing there, and then patted his pockets. He pulled his wallet from his pants and took out a five and handed it to her. She took it, but didn't move.

He closed the door in her face.

The sound of the latch and the deadbolt made her step back, but she could still hear the crying. Even through the door. Even over the sound of her pulse pounding in her ears. She put the money in her pocket.

She felt the ache build in her shoulders and shivered.

On the way to the bus stop she saw the door to Twelve was open. It was supposed to be empty. They only rented Twelve when everything else was dirty or full. The toilet always overflowed. She thought that it would serve Dwayne right if some squatters moved in and trashed the place, but then she remembered who would clean up that mess, and walked out of her way to close it. With her hand on the door knob, she felt a cool breeze across her wrist. She closed her eyes and told herself it was just the AC, and then pulled the knob until the lock clicked.

* * *

On the bus home she listened to her English lessons and tried to remember that America was the land of opportunity and not make a list of all the things she'd lost.

Juan was studying at the kitchen table when she got home. He started to pack his books.

"It's okay," she said.

"No, I know it makes you sad."

"We'll eat in the living room, watch tv."

His eyes narrowed. She never wanted to watch tv.

"I need the distraction," she said, her eyes flicked to the letter on the fridge but he didn't see. "Just not the news."

"No mail?" he asked, standing.

She shook her head.

"Did Dwayne do something?"

"No more or less than usual." She leaned back against the counter, picked at something sticky on the edge of the sink.

Juan's nose wrinkled, "find something extra gross?" He was surprisingly squeamish for a soon to be doctor.

"You could say that."

"You don't want to tell me?"

"You won't believe me."

"Oh," he said, rubbing his brow with his palm. "You know it's not that I don't believe you, you know, about before."

"You don't." She crossed her arms.

"You think you saw something. It's that I don't believe—"

"Me."

"—in visions." He braced his hands on the table. "What did you see today?"

"Nothing."

"Why are we arguing then?"

"I heard a baby that wasn't there."

"TV?"

"No."

"Could it have been an animal? Or a ringtone?"

"I know what a baby sounds like!"

"I know," he said, and then quieter, "I know."

"I'm a very intelligent person. I'm not prone to hysteria. I'm level headed and cynical. You're not the only one with a graduate degree."

"I know."

"So, stop," she said. "Stop making me feel like I'm crazy."

They ate with the TV on so they didn't have to talk about the things they didn't want to think about. Then he went back to the kitchen to study, and she let the nonsense on the TV drown out the voices in her head. It mostly worked. She did sit ups during commercials to keep occupied. Attempted the crossword puzzle in the newspaper to keep her hands busy, but when her chin kept hitting her chest, she walked down the hall, and passed the bedroom that they didn't use. She didn't poke her head in like she usually did. She didn't adjust the curtains or smooth the linens. She just went to the bathroom, brushed her teeth and washed her face, stripped off her disgusting work clothes and fell into bed.

• • •

She slept terrible. Woke up sore and irritated. She took a shower and counted the tiles while she scrubbed and rinsed. Juan handed her a cup of black coffee when she walked into the kitchen. His backpack was next to the door. He was going to the library to use the computer. All she did was work and yet they didn't have enough for even a computer. They'd given up so much. They'd been tricked by the promise of the American dream. She closed her eyes and buried her face in his shoulder.

It was Thursday, so she took the bus to the Clark's, and used the code to get into their garage. She paused her English lesson to listen at the door between the garage and the house to see if they'd remembered to crate their dog. She couldn't hear any scratching or yipping, which was a good sign. In the kitchen she grabbed her supplies and noticed that Mrs. Clark had switched brands again. The opposite of Dwayne, Mrs. Clark rarely finished a bottle before she tired of it, and threw it away. The new cleaner had a tropical scent. Lourdes liked it, it reminded her of home.

Lourdes didn't think any of wives of the families she worked for had jobs. She didn't know where they went, on the one morning every week when she cleaned their houses. At least one woman seemed to go to the gym a lot. Her laundry was full of workout clothes. One of the others had a lot of degrees framed on the wall. All of them had huge closets full of beautiful clothes. Vanities covered in sparkling bottles. Lourdes thought about her life, before, in Honduras. She had had workout clothes. She had degrees and expensive perfume.

She had just put the vacuum away, and pulled the buds from her ears before she went to scrub the second-floor hall bath (she'd dropped her last pair in the toilet by accident wearing them while bending over to brush the porcelain) when she heard it.

"Mama."

Her breath came so sharp it hurt, and her body stilled to listen. With an ache throbbing in her chest, she reached out for the wall to steady herself. Nothing, only the faint whir of the overhead fan. She took a deep breath, turned to the toilet and threw up. The visions were coming more often. At first, they had been so far apart that she wasn't sure what she was really seeing. She didn't think of them as signs, at first. As messengers. Now, it was unavoidable, and she was wound so tightly she was starting to fray. She cleaned the toilet, and the tub, and the sinks. She polished the mirror and avoided looking at her face, she knew what she would see. She knew what moving to this country had done to her complexion, to her body.

She was at the top of the stairs when she heard it again. Her knees went out and she sat down hard on the wood. She pinched the bridge of her nose. Was she as crazy as Juan thought? She took a deep breath and got to her feet. She searched the second floor, finding nothing, of course. She needed to get out, before she completely lost it. She rushed through the rest of her tasks, thankful that the house was already very clean and they wouldn't notice that she'd been distracted.

On her way back to the garage she heard it again, and this time found herself on her knees on the wood floor. It was close. She crawled to the utility room, where it sounded like the cry was coming from. She reached up and flipped the light. The dog, in its crate was looking at her. It whined. The sound was eerily similar.

Lourdes sighed.

She wasn't crazy.

• • •

On the bus to the motel she thought about all the possible explanations, again, for what she kept seeing. Her abuela would say it was susto. Lourdes needed to pray more. Maybe she should have some herbs. Her mama would try to sneak her to a curandero. Juan would tell her to think about all the weird noises their house in Tegucigalpa used to make when the wind came from the west. He would tell her to remember the shadows in their garden when the moon was waning. He would remind her that everything was scary when you were scared. And she would try to breathe deeply, and listen to his heart beating and forget what she'd seen.

But she couldn't help but wonder if these ghosts were angels. Like how Gabriel came to Mary to tell her the good news of her pregnancy. Maybe these strange sightings were warning that good news was coming, a mistake had been made, that they'd be using that second bedroom soon. Or that she just needed to hold on. She remembered the story of Daniel, and how the angel came to restore his strength. She could do that; she could be strong. She tried to forget about Lot and why the angels came to him.

• • •

She got off the bus and walked the three blocks to the motel. She pushed open the back door to the office and punched her card. She waved at Dwayne and was about to head back to get her supplies when she couldn't help herself, "did the guy in six check out yet?"

"Early, like 5am."

"He have a kid with him? A baby?"

"Not in here."

"Hmm," she said, already on the sidewalk, already on her way to six. She wasn't losing it. She was going to find something in that room that explained the sound.

She opened the door and stood in the middle of the silent room holding her breath. The bed was messed up, and there were towels in the bathtub, but she could find no evidence of a child, no pacifier under the bed, no tiny socks left behind a chair. She looked from the AC unit under the window to the television.

That must be it, she thought. She's sure she can remember that the TV was on. If he'd been watching TV, maybe not paying attention, maybe just to have some noise in the background, there could have been a baby. Maybe he didn't notice that there was a baby, maybe it was a commercial that just came on as he was running to the door.

"A commercial," she whispered to herself. Over and over, she whispered, as she went to the storage room, and pulled her cart out onto the sidewalk, and straight into Dwayne.

"Shit. Watch it, would ya. Where have you been?"

"Six," she said.

"He trash it?"

"No."

Dwayne narrowed his eyes. "You're acting weird again. Don't start with that visions shit. Don't get me wrong, I'd love some of those ghost TV wackos to think we're haunted, we'd fill these rooms every night. But you've got too much to do today. Make sure twelve gets done, too. Actually, do twelve first. We need everything open tonight and who the hell knows when the last time there was anyone in there. It's probably stuffy as hell."

"Yesterday."

"What?"

"Someone was in there yesterday."

He sighed loudly. "Get it together. A full house means you're a little bit closer to getting a new toy!" With that he slapped his hand against the side of her cart. It tipped and spilled toilet rolls and tiny soaps on the concrete. Dwayne walked away leaving Lourdes to pick them up herself.

On her knees on the ground she looked over to the door of twelve and shivered. It was just the AC, she told herself. It made the room cold. It changed the air pressure and popped the door. That's all. No visions. No ghosts. No angels. She wasn't crazy. She didn't need to be afraid, she thought. All the others could be explained, this would be, too. The mystery would be solved, and she would feel just the tiniest bit stupid, but that was okay, most people assumed she was stupid.

She stepped inside the room and the smell brought her to her knees. Baby shampoo. Milk breath. Lourdes pressed her forehead to the floor. She could feel the weight of her babies in her arms. She could hear their voices, their squeals, their cries. She ran her hands over her flattened breasts, her saggy belly. "They were here," she whispered. "I'm not crazy."

Behind her, Dwayne shouted. "Get up. What the hell?"

Lourdes sobbed into the carpet.

"Fucking shit. What's the matter with you?"

"Babies," she said.

"There are no babies in here. There is nothing in here. It's actually in way better shape than I was expecting. It's just a bit cold. That's a selling point, isn't it? I think so. Get off the floor. Go clean some rooms."

But she couldn't.

Lot, she thought. Lot. And she couldn't be here, at work, counting her steps, or conjugating verbs, or trying to remember Pythagorean theorem or order of operations to occupy her mind to keep it from wandering to that paper on the fridge, and what might be waiting in her mailbox right now. If these visions were a warning or gift she didn't know, but she couldn't go on until she did.

• • •

The bus ride home seemed unending. She stood in the lobby of her building in front of the mailboxes. The piles of sale papers on the floor told her it had been delivered. Her hand gripped the key, but shook as she turned it in the lock. She pulled the stack of letters out, tucked them under her arm, and relocked the box. She climbed the stairs to their apartment as fast as her feet would carry her, crashed through her front door, and spread the mail on the counter.

Bills. Not the letter they'd been waiting for.

She looked over at the fridge. At the old letter, folded and tacked to the side. She didn't need to read it. She'd memorized every word. Department of Homeland Security. Children. Detained. Missing. They'd lost her children. They'd stolen her whole world.

She ran to the spare room and fell to the floor between the two empty cribs. Remembered covering the twins with her body as the men with guns burst into their home in Honduras. Remembered nursing both of them on the never-ending bus ride north to the border. Each mile a tiny bit of hope rising; they were going to be safe, they were going to be okay. She remembered the pale skinned agents pulling babies from her arms as their family was separated, the babies' eyes wide, their lips quivering against the stranger's polyester uniform. She remembered the way that her breasts ached as her milk built in the absence of the mouths that needed them. How they burst and leaked, but eventually shriveled and dried, as she waited, day after day, week after week, and now, more than a year later, they hung empty, a reminder of this never-ending wondering, hoping, fearing.

"Please let me be Mary," she said to the ghosts in the corners. "Not Lot."

The Monster Beneath

Now - Spring 2018

Minna's mother set the mug on the scarred wooden table. Minna wrapped her cold hands around it. The mug was one her mother had made, but deemed unsellable. The glaze was the exact rich cobalt of Lake Superior on a July afternoon, but smoke had gotten in the kiln, adding blots of dark grey and black, hints at the danger beneath the waves. It was Minna's favorite mug. She looked to the basket where her mother kept the Coffeemate, and a bottle of maple syrup, and then stood to grab the sugar bowl from the buffet. Her sidearm caught against the edge of the table with a clatter.

Her mother winced.

"Sorry," Minna said and stirred four heaping spoonfuls of sugar into her brew.

"Someday that's going to catch up with you," her mother said, patting her farm wife hips. "Being the sheriff is a lot more pressure. It's hard on your heart."

"I'm not really the sheriff."

"Yet," her mother said and wiped a generous smear of butter on her pulla and took a bite.

"Interim," Minna said, and then smiled and said: "For now."

Minna's phone rang. It was her deputy. "We got a body," he said in his usual soft-spoken brevity. Her heart raced.

"One sec," she said into the phone as she stood, the chair screeching across the floor. "Sorry Mama," she mouthed as she ran out the side door, and across the slushy drive. "Okay, shoot," she said, every nerve in her body snapping and ready.

"Twenty-something female. Agawa Bay. Appears to have washed ashore. Puncture wounds on her leg. Perhaps an animal bite. Found about an hour ago by some local boys. We are securing the scene."

"Make sure they leave the body in position. I'm on my way." As Minna hung up and turned to open the driver's door, she was surprised to see her mother standing in the slush.

"A body?"

"Not him," Minna said. "Female."

Her mother nodded, and handed her a piece of bread wrapped in waxed paper. Minna hugged her mother, got in the truck, and then left her behind.

In Northern Michigan distance was measured not in miles but time. In twenty minutes, Minna would see her first dead body as Interim Sheriff, and only her fourth in the fifteen years she'd been on the force. But every time she wondered if it was him. And every time a body disappeared into the cold, dark of Lake Superior she wondered if it was Mishipeshu taking someone else.

Then - Fall 1991

Winter was near, fog clouded the window panes. Minna's daddy usually put plastic over them to keep out the cold, but he hadn't yet. A draft brushed her bare knees beneath the Michigan Tech t-shirt she stole from his drawer and wore to bed every night. Minna looked out to the sky darkening behind the trees, and wished she could see the lake beyond. She imagined watching her dad coming across the water in his new blue fishing boat, named after her; running downstairs and telling her mama and pappa that he was home. She'd had this wish for a week now.

"You're supposed to be in bed little one," Pappa said from the door. The light from the hall spilled warm around him into her darkened room. "Come now, I'll tuck you in."

Minna didn't want to sleep until Daddy came home.

"Come now, I'll tell you a story."

She turned at that, toward her grandfather, his hair sticking straight up from pulling off his toque. She got under the covers.

"When I was a little boy, almost exactly your age," he said, pulling a chair to the side of the bed, speaking low, more like a whisper.

"Tell me the one about the storm."

"Not tonight."

"Yes tonight. I want to hear a true story."

He said: "I only tell true stories. Now, your mother is going to be mad... Fine, fine, settle in. When I was a wee lad, I went fishing with my pa one morning before school. Mama didn't want us to go. She didn't like the look of the sky. She thought a storm was coming. My pa thought that it was hogwash, and that women were always worried about the sky. If it was raining, they'd holler about umbrellas and boots, snow it was toques and mitts, hell, even in the sun they went on about sunscreen and dehydration. They were never happy, he said, so he ignored her.

"It was cold, even for November. Windy, misty, like God was spitting, but we bundled up because we knew we only had a few of these mornings left before the bay iced over. It was still dark as my pa dropped anchor on our favorite spot, a little cove tucked beside a cliff. When I stood to cast my line, I noticed how wild the lake was, the waves were huge, even in that protected cove. The waves were so large that the boat rocked and we rubbed against the cliff wall, scratched the gunwale all up. Pa cursed. It started to rain harder, the water was getting under my hood. I was starting to think Mama was right, but couldn't say that. Instead, I said: "We should go back. I got to go to school." It was so dark, we still had the lantern on, and he went to argue with me but looked at his watch first. I remember how all of the color fell out of his face. It was much later than he thought. It was dark because of the weather. Not the time.

"Put your lifejacket on," he said. And then tried to start the boat but it wouldn't turn over. All I could think about was Jeffrey Smith, a boy in the grade above me. He had gone missing that summer. He and his dad had got caught out in a storm. Their boat was found days later, upside down on the rocks, but they never found Jeff or his dad. All anyone at school talked about was what it felt like to drown. If you'd be able to feel the water in your lungs, taking your breath. Or if the temperature of the water would make you numb, and you could just watch as you sunk to the bottom. Others were convinced that Mishipeshu took them, but everyone was afraid to talk of her, as if saying her name would summon her from the deep.

"I just watched the light bulb in the lantern and tried to ignore how many times my dad yanked that starter. We hit the cliff again. He made me hold an oar out to keep us off the rocks. I was trying, but I was all of 70 pounds then and that oar was heavy, and the wind and the waves - I'd never seen them like that before. I tried to hold on, but a bigger wave came, and stole my weight. I was airborne, and when I reached out so as to not end up in the water between the boat and the rocks, I dropped the oar. Then we had nothing but the two of us, two rods, a dead motor, and a lantern; and a lake that wanted to swallow us. I knew the next wave would be the last.

"I watched the swell of the dark water move toward us, charging like wild horses across a field.

"I watched the side of the boat rise in the air above my head.

"I turned to the space between the boat and the rock, the space that I should soon find my small body trapped in icy water, but there were scales there instead of water. And spikes. And eyes. Big, intelligent eyes that looked into mine as she held up the side of the boat.

"My dad had the pull start in his hand as he fell and it finally yanked hard enough to start the motor. As he drove the boat out of the cove, I tried to find her again, but I couldn't. I only got that one time. The time she saved my life."

"Do you think she saved my daddy?"

"I think she would if she could."

"And if she couldn't?"

"Then I think she took him down to her home in the very bottom of the lake and is taking very good care of him there."

"I wish you wouldn't fill her head with nonsense," said her mother from the door. "It's not like we aren't having a hard enough time without fairy tales."

"Mishipeshu is not a fairy tale," said Pappa. "I saw her and I'm not the only one."

"Minna, say night-night to Pappa. You've got school in the morning."

Minna rolled over so she could look out the window, stuck a piece of her white blonde hair into her mouth. Her mom and pappa were arguing in the hallway. Her mama never liked stories about what lived below the surface of the lake. She couldn't believe in things she couldn't see, she said, and that went for God and Mishipeshu or whatever, and she didn't think either of them had her husband.

Whenever Mama talked like that Minna put her fingers in her ears and pressed her tongue against the roof of her mouth and counted the ridges.

Her daddy was Sheriff Kokkenen. Her daddy was who you went to if your dog was missing, or if you got separated from your mom at the grocery store. He rescued people from burning car wrecks and found them lost in the snowy woods. He stopped bad guys and saved the day. He would come back to her; it was just a matter of when.

Now

Lake Superior has plenty of beautiful beaches, Agawa Bay was not one of them. It wasn't a surprise that a body would wash up there, the currents were strong, and the waves seemed to beat on the land even when the rest of the lake was calm. Minna climbed over the rocks and picked her way along the stony shore to meet her deputy, Rankin, and two medics.

"No footprints but the boys' when I arrived," Rankin said by way of greeting.

They hadn't had any new snowfall in days. The woman hadn't walked or been carried in. She'd washed ashore, and Minna could tell. She was soggy. Her naked body: white, gray, and purple, verging on translucent, except for the dark puncture marks in her mangled lower leg.

Minna squatted for a closer look. "Bear?" she asked, but knowing that her guess was off, the bite wider than a bear's muzzle, more like a fish, or a big cat.

"Looks more like a sturgeon," one of the medics said. "You know they pulled an eight-footer out over in Marquette just two weeks ago. She looks like she could have been in the water for more than two weeks. Minna stood, rubbed her outer arms, and then walked over to Rankin, who was taking pictures of everything.

"No local girls missing. Send these pics to the state cops and see who she is. Get these guys to pack her up to the ME then I guess we wait our turn for news. About all we can do," she said and then nodded to the medics who slid the woman onto the backboard and carried her to their vehicle. Minna looked out to the water and shivered.

"You want me to check with the Canadians?" Rankin asked.

"That's a good idea. Jesus, I wonder what happened to her leg. The ME will have to tell us if the water killed her or not, but that leg… fuck, those wounds say that that horror happened when she was alive."

"I know what you're thinking."

"I know you do. Don't worry, I won't say it out loud. I won't tank my career before it starts. But seriously, doesn't it look like it?"

Rankin was trying to hide a small smile when Minna's stomach growled loudly.

"You headed home for dinner then?" Rankin asked.

"Nah. Chris is meeting the realtor."

"I don't know if I told you how sorry I am for your loss?"

"You did. Thanks." She turned and smiled at him. "I think I'm going to look around a bit and see if anything else has washed up."

"I'll help."

"You go home to your girls. I know they'll be missing you."

Deputy Rankin, frowned the way he always did when she said something like that. Something meant to be nice but served as a reminder of her heartbreak. She looked over at him and smiled. "Go," then chuckled, "that's an order."

"You're going to start that now, eh?"

"Nah." She smiled again, looking across the lake, trying to hear his footsteps over the crash of the surf. He was notoriously light-footed, and one of the few people in this town she could trust. Only six weeks ago they had been equals, before her father-in-law died and left the Sheriff's desk empty, and she took the interim position. Rankin was a better police officer, she knew. Better at procedure. Better with people. There was a sense of calm and safety about him. Maybe it was his size. Maybe his stillness. Maybe the kindness in his brown eyes. But Minna had the questions. She was suspicious. Pushy. He comforted victims. She caught perps. So, she got the promotion and the support from the department to run.

She had so many questions. Who was this woman? Whose daughter? Wife? Mother? How long had she been in the water? How did she get there? What happened to her leg? Minna hoped she was dead before the water got her. Minna had spent a lot of time in the last years thinking about what it would be like to bob in the middle of the lake, with no land in sight, just flat blue as far as she could see. To bob until she couldn't tread any longer, until her muscles gave out, and then that sinking, sucking, feeling as the water absorbed her.

It was anyone's guess how long the ME would take to get her answers, their backwater county not being high priority. All she would have for now is what she could pull together, and as interim sheriff all eyes were on her. Her father-in-law had been beloved: smart and kind, he'd bend over backwards for victims and their families. She was filling big shoes.

The grey water was dotted with icebergs. The ice on the bay had only been broken for a week. She wondered if the woman had been trapped under it. If the coming of spring, the warming water, had brought her to the surface. If she wasn't looking for a woman who just went missing.

She turned from the water and looked at the spot on the beach where the body had been. She wished she'd had Rankin's pictures. The woman had looked good, but Superior was so cold. Perhaps her leg injury was from the pack ice. The sharp ice that pushed and stacked on each other like tectonic plates along the beach could certainly destroy a leg. This was a theory she could bring to the public, one that didn't involve mythic creatures from the bottom of the lake.

She squatted next to the outline of the body, the footprints of her coworkers, the flat slide of the backboard a ring in the snow. Remembering the splay of the woman's limbs, the purple of her lips and fingers, she promised the woman that she would solve this mystery. She wouldn't leave this woman's family wondering. She was about to stand when a glint caught her eye. She leaned closer; a shard of metallic grey was lodged in the stones that had been beneath the woman's damaged leg. She pulled gloves from her pocket and picked it up. It looked like a piece of a saw blade, or a shark's tooth. She put it in a plastic baggie. She searched the rest of the woman's impression but found no other foreign matter.

Minna stood on the shore, listening to the wind whistle past her ears, looking down at the gray triangle in her hand, and thought about the pictographs of the water lynx on the cliffs across the lake. She wasn't the first one to consider this beast.

She thought of its sharp teeth, and claws, and the spikes that graced its back and remembered yet again why she stayed out of the deep.

Then

Snow was falling from the flat grey sky in fat clumps. They stuck to Minna's eyelashes as she lifted her face and stuck out her tongue to catch them.

"Is that supposed to be Mishipeshu?" Chris asked, brushing his mittens together and stepping away from his snowman version of Gordie Howe.

"Yep, but I can't get the spikes on her back to stand up."

"We could knock some of the icicles off the garage and use those."

The two kids charged over to the garage and stared up at the jagged ice dangling from the roofline.

"There's got to be a stick, a shovel, or something in the garage that we can knock them down with," he said.

They went into the garage and while Chris looked for something with a long handle, Minna looked up to the rafters.

"What about that," she said pointing high up on the wall.

"My grandpa's old saw. He and his brother used it to clear this land. They each held the side and yanked."

"It's perfect," Minna said. "I want a closer look." She turned over a bucket and used it to climb up onto the freezer. The saw looked exactly like the water lynx' spine in her mind, long and flexible.

"That would look cool," he said, climbing up beside her.

"What the hell are you two doing?" Chris's dad asked from the door. He was still in his uniform. His new sheriff badge winked at Minna and she swallowed hard. "Minna sweetheart come down from there," he said, holding his arms out to her so she could jump. "You two know not to play around freezers. This one locks on its own. If you ever ended up inside you wouldn't get out. And Jesus, Chris you know that, how many times have I told you these aren't toys. You could lose your hand if you touched them wrong," he hollered pointing at the collection of traps hanging from the wall. Minna knew not to touch them. Her dad had some at home. She had seen him catch a coyote once. Her stomach turned at the thought of the sounds that animal had made before Daddy shot him.

"Minna, sweetheart, can you go get in the cruiser? Another person's gone missing, and it's not safe for you to be out. I'm going to take you back to your mom on my way back to work. Chris, you go on inside. Your mother is waiting."

Minna climbed into the passenger seat of the cruiser. There was a paper bag sitting on the floor with a loaf of bread sticking out of the top.

"Buckle up," he said. "That's for you and your mama, okay?" he pointed at the bag. Chris' daddy's car was just the same as her daddy's, but it smelled of cologne and peppermints, while her daddy's smelled like salt and Christmas trees.

"I know your mama is really angry right now, and she has every right to be. And I know that she doesn't want to talk to me. But you know if you ever need anything you just call, eh? Your daddy was my best friend, and I'll do anything for you."

"Is," she said.

"Sorry, love?"

"Is your best friend. He'll be home soon."

Now

The bell above the door jangled as Minna stepped into Pour Boys and knocked the slush off her boots. John was behind the bar. He waved, and pointed towards the back corner. She nodded her thanks. Chris was waiting for her, a Bell's in front of him, and a Coke waiting for her. She knew as soon as she sat, Susie, John's wife, would put plates of fried walleye and french fries in front of them. Her stomach grumbled with anticipation. She'd spent a long day looking for more grey triangles on the beach, and leaving harassing voice messages for the ME. She slid into the booth and smiled at her husband.

"Hey baby," he said, putting his phone down. "Found Mishipeshu?"

"I'm not in the mood to be poked."

Chris raised his eyebrows. Normally she would smile, but she was too tired.

"I'm being serious," he said. "You know we've talked about this for decades, you know how I feel."

"I know. Sorry. It's just," she pulled her phone out of her pocket and swiped at the screen, "look at that bite on her leg. It's not a bear. It's not a sturgeon either."

Chris handed back her phone as Susie set the plates down. Minna was sure to tip the screen away from the waitress, aware that not everyone talked about bodies and wounds over dinner. Except maybe the interim sheriff, and the son of the former sheriff, who was also a world-class rescue diver.

"There's nothing in that bay that would have made those marks. That's for sure," he said, shoving fish into his mouth. "But we both know that there's plenty of predators out there."

Minna squeezed lemon on her fish, and bit her lip. He was right. She could have got that injury on land, but Lake Superior was full of secrets. Anyone who spent any real time on the water had stories, experiences that couldn't be explained any way other than a fantastic beast. Fisherman, and sailors on freighters came to town with tales of boats being bumped, nets with holes larger than any fish ever caught. Her father had no respect for the environmentalists, but they had stories too of mutilated animal remains, fish and wildlife with horrible injuries. Every local family had a story. The lore ran deep. These bites were pointing to Mishipeshu, but would the beast have given this woman up? How had she gotten away? How was Minna going to explain her theory to the other officers and not get laughed out of town?

"How are you?" she said. "House cleaning still? Need some help?"

"God, he was a pack rat, there's something in every corner, every drawer is full of shit, from fishing lures to old mittens to receipts from lunches decades ago that I'm sure he had with your dad. Trophies and certificates, and pictures, so many pictures. But no, it's okay, it's kind of cathartic, saying goodbye to things he loved, things that meant something to him; getting to revisit all these memories, just me and him." He took a bite and chewed. "It will be really nice to get the house on the market and off our hands though. Clean slate, you know?"

Things hadn't been easy the last couple of years. Working for her father-in-law was a challenge, but he'd always been good to her. She suspected out of his love for her father, maybe out of guilt that he hadn't been able to find him or save him. She knew though that he'd hoped that Chris would do something bigger with his life. He hated him poking around the bottom of the lake, he said. Hated that they entertained the idea of Mishipeshu and called them old fashioned. "What's that?" she said pointing at a package sitting next to Chris in the booth.

"New weight belt," he said. "Getting too thick in the middle for my other one."

Her phone vibrated on the table. It was the ME. She didn't even wipe the grease from her fingers before she answered. But when the doctor gave her the news, it wasn't at all what she was expecting.

"You look like you've seen a ghost." Chris said as she put down the phone.

"I sort of have."

"What?" he said, laughing, taking a drink of his beer. "And people think we're crazy for believing in a water panther."

She shook her head. "It's the woman. They identified her. She's been missing for 30 years. It's her, Chris. It's the woman that disappeared when my dad did. Chris, everyone always said that they had been together. What if he's out there too?"

Then

Minna lay on the end of the dock peering down into the lake. There was ice on the wooden planks, and surrounding the post that went down into the water, but it would be more than a month before this bay would freeze. She had time.

"What are you doing kiddo?" Pappa asked, standing over her. "This isn't a safe place for you to be hanging out. I know you're a good swimmer, but your snowsuit and this cold water don't mix."

"I'm being careful. I need to see."

"See what?" he said, and bent over, looking into the water. "What is that down there? An anchor?"

"Coyote trap."

"What? How do you know? How did that get there?"

"I couldn't find the bear traps."

"You put that down there? Jesus, Minna! Someone is going to get really hurt."

"Not in the winter. No one's going down there in the winter. Except Mishipeshu. We're going to catch her, and then ask her where she took my dad."

"Oh Minna!"

"You said that's why we couldn't find him, because he was with her. That's why Lake Superior never gives back its dead. It's because of her, and I want him back"

Now

Minna pulled into the rutted drive and wished she'd brought Rankin with her. He was so much better at this kind of stuff than her. He knew what to say to grieving families. She just seemed to make it worse. But the notification was an hour from the station and they both couldn't be gone that long just for this. Someone had to hold down the fort. She closed the truck door and stamped her boots on the ground to warm her feet. A man came out of the open garage door.

"Can I help you?" he asked, his eyes running over her uniform.

"Are you Rebecca Whitefish's next of kin?"

"That's my mom. Did you find her?"

"Yes," she said.

"Wow," he said, stepping back into the garage and leaning on the edge of a saw horse. "I didn't expect that, not after all this time, not this way." He rubbed his face with his hands. "Wait. I heard on the news a body washed up on the beach, that's not her, is it? It can't possibly be, thirty years in the water…"

Minna nodded. "That's what we are investigating now. I'm sorry I don't have more answers. Will let you know, as soon as we know, but I thought you'd want the closure of at least knowing—"

"That she's dead. She isn't living in Detroit or Minneapolis. That's what the police tried to tell my grandfather."

"Can I speak to your grandfather?"

"He's dead, too."

"I'm very sorry to hear that," she took a deep breath. "And I'm very sorry that the police at the time were not helpful as they could have been. I know there was a lot going on for them."

"It's not real comforting when your mom is missing though, yeah? Shit," he said and leaned harder into the sawhorse.

Minna turned to give him a minute to pull himself together and noticed a boat in the back of the garage covered with a tarp. Sky blue boat. A boat exactly the same color as her eyes.

"Where'd you get that?" she asked

"Sheriff gave it to my grandpa. Said it was to help with his environmental protection projects. Grandpa knew it was a bribe, or a warning maybe for him to stop making trouble with his protests."

"Protests?"

"All the waste from the paper plant used to be dumped into the lake. Decimated the fish population, which drove the predators into town because they're starving, but that's an excuse to trap those big beautiful beasts, isn't it? Anyway, because of my grandpa they don't dump or trap wolves or bears anymore."

"Which sheriff?"

He shrugged. "What does it matter?"

"After your mom went missing?"

He shrugged again. "I wasn't there. Mighta been before. Grandpa had a lot of run-ins with 'em. I just keep it because the police gave it to us, and they never did nothing else for us. Seems like maybe that means something."

"Can I look in there?" she asked.

His eyes narrowed. "You have a warrant?"

"It could be a crime scene."

"I don't think the police would give us a crime scene? Do you?"

He was right, there wouldn't be any blood evidence in there. She just wanted in to soothe the ache inside her. Maybe it would still smell like him. Maybe there would be some of his things. Her mother had been so angry, she hadn't kept anything.

"I'd like to see in it."

"No. I don't want you to find some reason to take it."

She could reveal herself. She could tell him that she was an orphan, too. That she was angry at the police, too. That she also lived in a state of constant hope that made her brittle and fragile. She could lay claim to this boat, but she'd compromise everything. She'd get a warrant. She'd come back.

She nodded, "I'm sorry for your loss. I'll be in touch with any further developments." She looked at the blue boat one more time. The one she knew said "Minnow" on the back, above the motor, and then she left wondering whether it was her dad, or her father-in-law who gave the boat away, if her mother knew, and if this was why her father-in-law and mother hated each other.

Then

Despite the cold weather, Minna was sunburned. Her cheeks felt hot and tight. The feeling reminded her of fishing with her dad. She swallowed hard. They were headed back to land with a cooler full of fish. It had been a good day.

"I wish we were in your dad's boat," Chris shouted over the loud motor. "It's so much faster and nicer than my dad's. I just want to go home and eat."

"Yeah," she said, but she wasn't paying attention, she was scanning the surface of the water for swirls, or lumps, or anything out of the ordinary. Anything that could be the monster that took her father. And gripping the gunwale. She'd never been afraid of the deep water before, but when she looked down all she could imagine was beasts, lurking.

Chris's dad docked the boat, and the kids raced to shore to pee and warm up and then watch Inspector Gadget on the basement TV while the grown-ups dealt with the fish. Minna loved Penny. Chris said they looked alike. This was her favorite show, but she couldn't concentrate. She was so angry at her pappa for pulling that trap out of the water.

"You still thinking about Mishipeshu?"

"Always. I've realized I can't catch her, though. I have nothing big enough to get her inside. So, I'm going to bait her, if I could just get a picture of her, I'd have enough proof. Someone would believe me, and help."

"You just got to get a pile of fish. We could catch them."

"I can get it from the garbage at the market. My dad used to get his bait from there for his traps."

"You're gonna be just like Penny," Chris said.

She smiled, crossed her arms and sunk into the couch to watch the end of the episode.

"Minna," Chris's dad called down the stairs to the basement. "Time to go home sweetie and take that container with you, okay? Some of the fish we caught today."

"I don't know why you're sending so much." Chris's mom said. "It's just the three of them. Put the extra in the freezer in the garage."

"Because," Chris's dad said widening his eyes, "I'm not sure how she's paying the bills right now, you know."

"I'm not sure he's not in that kiln of hers. Have you checked there? The woman is a first-class bitch."

Minna hated when adults talked about her like she wasn't there, and since her dad disappeared it happened more and more. Rumors and guesses about where he'd gone, rhetorical questions about how the family was holding up, or making ends meet. But today it didn't matter. Minna had a bag of fish so big she could barely lift it, and she couldn't believe her luck.

Now

Minna was parked at the county boat launch, watching the water, remembering the look on her mother's face thirty years before when her father pulled that blue boat on its trailer into their yard. Disbelief, and then anger, and then screaming. He'd spent all their money, and money they didn't have. It had been the subject of a hundred arguments in the weeks preceding his disappearance. She was wondering how to ask her mother if she'd known about Rebecca's family having the boat when the ME's office called. She punched her steering wheel, and drove straight to the office. She needed Rankin's calm head, she was losing hers.

"Frozen," she said, slapping the desktop. "Fucking frozen like a goddamn lasagna."

"The water is very cold. The ice is just breaking up. She was probably trapped in the pack just like you thought."

"No like frozen in someone's freezer." She skimmed through the report on her phone while she talked. "Fish scales, deer DNA, and residues that are consistent with the plastic interior of a freezer."

"So not commercial then? Are most of them metal?"

"Jesus Christ. Some regular person had this woman in their home freezer for thirty years. And, and the punctures are from a bear trap." She collapsed into her desk chair. "You know the rumor right? Rebecca and my dad ran away together. That they took his boat and started a new life somewhere else, but instead her family has his boat and she's in a freezer."

"You think maybe her family didn't want them to be together, killed them both and hid the boat? Made up some story about it being a gift. It's a really generous gift."

Her head was hot, her stomach doing somersaults. Rankin continued: "Minna, what would your mom have done if she found out your dad gave that boat away?"

She rested her head on the desktop. She was thinking about her mother, and what she would have done if she'd found the two together. She couldn't imagine her mother not selling the boat if she had the chance, certainly she wouldn't give it to her husband's mistress. Her mother had been so angry for so many years. She'd been sure that her husband had abandoned them for that woman. Minna couldn't imagine the energy it would have taken to fake that. She knew her mother didn't have it. Minna felt a loosening in her neck muscles, relief. That left her father, and Chris'. She had a hard time imagining her father giving away his boat, he'd been so proud of it, but maybe if he'd run out of money, maybe Rebecca's son had been mistaken and his grand-father had bought the boat to use for his protests. Minna found herself wishing that the answer was as easy as Mishipeshu. It was so much simpler when she was a child and had something to blame, one easy target for her anger.

"What's our next step?" Rankin asked quietly. He would sug-gest action of course. "A warrant for the boat? Canvassing? Or waiting for more information on the metal?"

Minna lifted her head as her gut tightened into a knot. "I know whose freezer she's been in," she said. "I just need to know why."

Then

Chris was standing at her front door with an ice auger.

"I can't. I'm grounded."

"Still?"

"Still."

"Over the fish?"

"Yep. Wasting food, two weeks. Huge mess, two weeks."

"God, your mom is mean. You're grounded til Christmas! I thought we could go drill some holes and set some traps."

"I'm not allowed out."

"Am I allowed in?"

Minna thought back to her mother's red-faced instructions. She hadn't said anything about Chris coming over, and she wasn't home, and Pappa was asleep in front of the hockey game.

"Sure, but be quiet," she said and they tiptoed to her room and closed the door.

Chris pointed to her dad's work hat, laying on her bed. "You really miss him, eh?"

Minna picked up the hat and smelled it. "Yeah. And I'm going to be police when I grow up so I can find him. So, I've been wearing it to practice."

"Don't you think Mishipeshu has him? My dad's trying, he's working overtime, he's never home and he's crying a lot. My mom tells him he's working too much. I know if your dad was out there on land he'd find him."

"My mom says he left with that woman. Took his new fancy boat and his new fancy woman and split. So, I'll be like Inspector Gadget and find them. Plus, I can't look down the bottom of the lake, it's too deep."

"I could," he said. "I'd do that for you."

"It's so deep," she said. "It's dark and cold and she's down there, and people who go down there don't come back. I don't want you..." She burst into tears.

He wrapped his arms around her. "I'll do it right," he said. "I'll look and I'll come back. I'll find the answer. You don't have to do it alone."

Now

At first, she thought no one was there. His truck wasn't in the driveway. She was relieved that she was wrong, but then she opened the side door to the garage and found it, and Chris. He was wearing rubber gloves. The room smelled of bleach.

"Is my dad in that freezer?" she said, pointing to his father's game freezer.

He shook his head.

"Was he?"

Chris looked down at his hands. He nodded.

"Where is he now?"

"With Mishipeshu."

"What?"

"She was the first and I messed up. I thought she would sink and she didn't. I should have weighted her."

"But you knew better for the second time."

He nodded.

"How long have you known? Since we were kids?"

"No."

"I'm such a fool. I trusted your dad. I trusted you. You're the one who encouraged me to think it was that fucking monster all these years. And you knew!"

"No! I didn't. Not till Dad started to get sick. He knew he was going to die and his position was going to be open and he wanted me to join the police so I could run for it, and continue his legacy, but I didn't want to. I'm happy diving. I love it. He told me I was doing it out of loyalty to you, out of some misplaced sense of duty to a stupid fairy tale that you convinced me of, and that you were just as dumb as your father. And then he told me.

"Your dad and Rebecca weren't together. It was mine. He loved her. He was going to leave my mom. Your dad was trapping bears for their parts. For the money. That's how he could afford that boat. Rebecca came from a family of conservationists. One night she went out in the woods to disable his traps, to ruin them, and she stepped in one. Our dads were together when they found her dead, your dad wanted to cover it up, wanted to bury her where he buried the remains of the bears. But my dad loved her and was so mad at your dad, and his stupid, greedy, traps, and what happened, that he killed your dad, and put both the bodies in the freezer. I'm so sorry Minna. I had no idea. When we were kids, he was so devastated, he was a mess, drinking all the time. I thought it was because your dad was missing. I had no idea it was this. I would have told you. Fuck, I wouldn't have spent my life searching the bottom of the lake."

Chris leaned against his truck. Pulled a rubber glove off and rubbed his hand through his hair. "But I kind of understand. If he loved her even half as much as I love you, I would kill anyone who hurt you, even my best friend.

"He was so ashamed. I think he would have taken the secret to his grave. He probably only told me because he was too weak to move the bodies and he knew he was going to be found out anyway. He probably wanted to defend himself. But what he did, it's indefensible. And all I've ever wanted was you, to protect you, to take care of you. I didn't want you to carry this. I thought this was better."

Minna watched his fingers, his hands, and how they grasped each other as he spoke, pleading for her to understand. How over the years, with those hands, he had held her, protected her, and helped her. She thought about how he pulled the flesh of Rebecca, and her father from the freezer with those same fingers. How he had loaded them into his truck and then into a boat all by himself. All the work and care it would have taken, the burden that he had carried. How he had done it for her, to save her the pain of knowing how stupid her father's end had been. And she hurt for him, knowing not only had his father put him in this terrible position of knowing, but he had also stolen Chris' lifelong dream to find the monster in the water; instead, he'd been living with the monster all this time.

But still her trust had been broken, and she needed to know. She needed to see for herself.

"Take me," she said. "Take me down in the water where you dropped him. I need to see him."

"Minna, no. That's a terrible idea. It's so deep where I dropped him and you're a beginner and you're afraid of the deep. We won't be able to go far enough down to find him."

"I have to try. Thirty years, Chris. I've waited thirty years."

He sighed, and nodded, and they got their gear, and Chris' boat, and he brought her out to the deepest point of the lake. "It's 1,300 feet here. You can only go about fifty. So please don't expect anything."

"Maybe he got caught on something," she said, put in her mouthpiece and tipped backwards into the water.

It was breathtakingly cold. Every muscle in her body contracted into a hard ball. She pushed through the cramps, trying to enjoy the quiet and the rhythm of her breath, trying not to think about the darkness below.

Chris signaled her and they began to descend slowly, her heart breaking a little with each foot of open water. It wasn't until she was nearing her limit of fifty feet that she saw rocky outcroppings. She pushed on. She could see Chris signaling, but she ignored him. More and more rocks appeared in the beam of her flashlight, but she saw nothing suspicious. It was darker and colder than she'd ever been, and she was angry and disappointed. She was just about to stop and return to the surface when she saw a flash of red in her beam, red like Chris' old weight belt, and she kicked down toward it, but it was gone. She kept descending, looking, sure she'd seen it. Pain built in her ears. Sparkles emerged in her vision, and she finally stopped. She'd lost Chris in her frantic swimming and was alone in the dark.

The weight of the lake was pressing down on her. Plus the weight of the knowledge of what their fathers had done, and the heavy realization that finding her father and knowing for sure was a lost cause; Superior didn't give up her dead.

She should swim, but her limbs wouldn't obey and she was so very tired.

She dropped the flashlight.

As it descended, the falling beam shining through the black water caught the flash of scales, and spines, and big intelligent eyes.

Glass Houses

E m peeled her right eye open. Her left was crusted shut and pressed into the sweaty pillowcase. Clothes and dirty towels covered every horizonal surface, and the stationary bike that she told Toya would never get used. She just couldn't bring herself to open the half-filled drawers or look at the empty side of the closet in order to put them away. *What did it matter?* Sunlight, burning through the blinds she forgot to close before she fell into bed this morning told her it was late afternoon, much too early to be awake, and yet, she was.

Why?

She had at least a couple more hours, and she could use days. *Was it because of last night?* Was it anxiety? Or relief? Was she awake because what had been building had finally come to a head? Because she had, as they'd all expected, finally fucked everything beyond fixable? She closed her eyes. Then she heard it, a knocking. Again, a pounding. It echoed through the empty house, vibrated in her belly. Then again.

"Goddamn girl scouts."

She pulled the pillow over her head.

Again.

"Fuck me." She rolled out of bed, stumbled down the hall, and threw open the front door.

"They've gone," said Travis, too loudly. Travis, who was maybe nine? Skinny, awkward, the boy who lived next door, who Em had only spoken to a handful of times because his parents thought she was everything that was wrong with the world. His face was pale, but his nose was red and his eyes were wide and full of water.

"What?" she said, pushing greasy, damp hair out of her face.

"Gone!" he shouted, near hysteria. "Without me!"

"Come in, come in." She sighed, rubbed her eyes, and beckoned to him. Resigned to the fact now that she would not be getting back to bed anytime soon. "Just come in and sit, okay?"

"No."

"What do you mean, no? You need to calm down. You need to explain what the fuck you're talking about so I can help you."

"That's a bad word."

"What?!? Oh…" Em rested her forehead against the door jamb. "What do you want?"

He chewed on his fingernail and looked up at the sky. "Is everyone gone?"

"Obviously not," she said. "I'm here."

"Right, but you're…" his cheeks took color and he looked at the ground.

"About out of patience." She looked at her watch. "I have to get back on my rig soon. I have to save people's lives." *That was kind of a stretch.* She was likely to spend her shift grounded behind a desk or in her supervisor's office after last night. "I need to be alert. So, I need some sleep. So, you need to tell me how I can help you, or you to go home to your mother and bother her."

"I told you, she's not home."

"Dad, then."

"Not him either. You're not listening."

Things were getting clearer. "They are probably just running late. It's okay. Don't you have a key? You're old enough to be home alone for a bit."

"The car is in the driveway."

Em leaned out and peered into their driveway, he was right.

"Maybe they went for a walk, you have a baby sister, right? They probably took her for a walk."

He shook his head.

Em's eyes hurt. Her teeth felt rough and her mouth tasted sour. "Have you gone inside?"

He nodded.

"They aren't there?"

He sighed and banged his fist against the side of the house.

"No note?" she asked.

He slapped his hand against his forehead. "Don't you listen, like, at all? They are gone. Forever. Without me." He sniffed and tears welled in his eyes. "They got called and I didn't," he whispered.

"Got called, what? They wouldn't leave you intentionally. Don't think like that. We don't even know where they are. They probably ran out on an errand. People get caught in traffic, get held up all the time. They are probably panicking too, trying to get back to ya."

"They're gone," he said. "I knew this would happen. I knew I'd be left behind. I've always known I wasn't good enough."

• • •

Em thought back to the first time she'd met his parents. She'd been in her uniform, arriving home after a long shift. They'd been carrying boxes from a moving truck across the overgrown lawn and into the neighboring house. Travis' mother was cute. She looked exactly like what a mom should look like, a collection of soft circles with a huge smile, and when she saw Em she waved and ran across the yard, hand extended.

"We're new!" she said, laughing. "I'm so glad we're neighbors!" she nodded at Em's uniform. "And you're a paramedic! That's so handy! I'm clumsy and bad with medical stuff. I'm always running into things, and the kid got that from me. Last time my little guy got a bonk on his noggin, I just about passed out. So, I'm so glad to have someone who knows what they are doing next door!"

"I'm happy to help," Em'd said. Pleased to have new people about her age next door. The previous owner had been elderly, and the house was in poor repair. Em felt like a jerk that she'd cared more about her property values than Old Mr. Booker's ability to live in his home, but she did.

"This is my boy," the woman said, "and my husband" as a little boy with his mom's dark curls and an average looking man came over.

"Hi there," the man said, and took off his sunglasses and held out his hand. "I'm Tim. Nice to meet you." Em thought that together they looked like a catalogue advertisement. Bland. Safe. He shook her hers and nodded toward the ring on her left hand. "Is your husband around? I'd love to meet him? Maybe get his help, the missus here isn't all that good with heavy stuff."

"Wife," Em said. "She's at work, and also not all that helpful with heavy stuff."

"Oh," the man and the woman said. Eyebrows raised. Mouths turned down. The wife put her hands on the boy's shoulders and pulled him against her abdomen. "I see," said the man, putting his glasses back on.

• • •

They just about ran away. Em shook her head. She'd had hope there for a moment, hope that the new people might be a little more open minded than Mr. Booker. Wasn't the world supposed to be changing? All the folks like her new neighbors kept complaining about how liberal everyone was getting, how we'd all moved away from their traditional family values. Em thought that was horseshit. If the world was getting more progressive, certainly there would be fewer of these idiots. She'd smiled thinking about swinging by the bakery the next day picking up a little welcome treat, and then stopping by their place with LaToya. She'd wondered what they'd think about that. The past few months they'd been extra annoying with worker guys coming and going all the time, the sound of hammers and saws screaming while Em tried to sleep. She just kept reminding herself that it could be worse, it could still be Mr. Booker next door. It could be a terrible smell wafting over from his dark and silent house, and not construction noise and children's laughter.

Travis clapped his hands to get her attention. She wondered what adult in his life did that.

"I know where they are," he said.

She wanted to lay down and close her eyes. She could be sleeping. She could be working on forgetting her disastrous last shift, the warning, and all the texts on her phone from LaToya.

"What do you need then, a ride?"

"You can't drive me to heaven."

Em's mouth went dry.

"What the fuck? Why would you say that?" *Dear God, dear God, dear God.* She screamed in her head. *What did he see? What did he do?*

"Mom said, if I ever woke up in the night and they weren't there, or if I came home from school and they were missing, that I shouldn't worry because they were with Jesus and everything was going to be okay."

What a monster this woman was. Em knew that they had some opposing political views, but this… she sat heavily on the top step of the porch. Travis sat beside her.

"So, are they always home when you come home from school? They are never gone to the grocery store, or been even just a minute or two late?"

He shook his head.

She thought about her own mother. She usually tried not to. Sometimes she couldn't get past the petty feeling that her mother cared about what the other biddies in her book club thought more than anything else. That she honestly didn't care who Em was fucking, but her Sunday School class did. Em let the anger and resentment that all those women were allowed to love and support their daughters no matter how many marriages fell apart, no matter how many babies were born out of wedlock. That the alcoholic, cheating, gambling, gluttonous, shopaholic daughters were allowed to have relationships with their families, but the lesbians raised in the church had to leave.

Other times, she felt more gracious, and she realized it wasn't easy to have your child be the embodiment of everything you fear. Em couldn't help but think about the mothers of serial killers, of rapists and murderers, though. How many of them she'd seen on TV or in interviews over the years? How many of them still deeply loved their children? How many of them could see past the sin and still love the sinner, and that sin was violence and assault. Surely a girl kissing a girl wasn't as bad. Wasn't there a hierarchy of sins? Wouldn't that leather-bound fairytale her mother kept by her bedside say that abandoning one's child was at least just as bad as a little girl on girl? And probably worse? How did longing to rest her head on LaToya's soft breast make her a bad person? Em realized that the nonsense that had come from Travis' mother's mouth could have easily come from her own mother and her stomach tightened and rolled.

"How often do you worry about coming home to an empty house?" she said.

"Everyday."

"Shit." She rubbed her sore face. "What are you supposed to do? What the plan?"

He shrugged. She sighed. The sun was falling. She needed to figure this out before she was late to work. She was already on thin ice, if not an iceberg heading for a waterfall. "Why don't we go over there and look around? Do your grandparents live nearby?"

"My aunt lives in Atlanta."

"Well," she said, and stood. Her body ached, her muscles tired and sore. "What did you see when you went in before?"

"Nothing. I ran around downstairs, shouted. I didn't have to see anything. I knew. I could feel it."

• • •

Em, too, could feel it when she walked in. She could smell it too, blood and feces. "Stay down here, Travis. Look for a phonebook, or something with your Aunt's number on it."

The main floor of the house was empty. Em prayed that she wasn't about to find what she thought she was going to find. She'd been an EMT for fifteen years. She knew what death smelled like. The scent got stronger as she climbed the stairs. A bedroom with pale blue walls, a desk, and a baseball glove on the floor, empty. Next was pink walls, crib. Empty. *Thank you, Jesus.* The door at the end of the hall was only open a crack. She put her hand inside her t-shirt and used it to push open the door.

Sometimes, she really hated being right.

Three bodies. Two on the bed naked. Gunshot wounds to chests and abdomens. Travis' mom, and the carpenter. They'd been working on Mr. Booker's decades of neglect. They were settling in, making a life.

Another man, facedown, in the corner. Clothed. She prayed it wasn't Tim; that he was somewhere else with the baby. Prayed that Travis had someone out there.

She turned the body over. It was Tim. She recognized his mouth, his nose. He had a revolver trapped under his body, and was bleeding from his temple. He'd fallen on the baby. Em pulled her out hoping that she'd just been trapped. Hoping she'd been spared or forgotten.

But she hadn't.

Em wondered if her death has been revenge or mercy. It wasn't hard to tell what had happened here. She'd thought these types of people were supposed to be immune from this kind of thing. The order of the shots was unclear for now, and that made her chest ache. The techs would figure it out later, but Em didn't want to know. She didn't like Travis' mother, she didn't like her snide comments about all the bottles in Em's recycling after LaToya left, she didn't like her political signs or her scrunched nose whenever Em and LaToya had friends over. But Em wouldn't wish the torture of watching your child die on any mother. She backed out of the room and called 911 from her cell phone. She kept her voice down.

After hanging up, she led Travis out to the porch to wait. She looked at her watch yet again.

"Do you know those neighbors?" She asked, pointing to the tidy house on the other side. More old people, she could see a face watching them in the kitchen window.

"Yeah. They go to my church."

"So… why did you come to my house then?"

"Mom said you wouldn't be raptured."

"Cause I'm a lesbian?"

"Well, that and…"

"And what?"

"What happened to your hand? Your face? Did you get hurt at work? My mom talked about your job a lot. She said maybe I should be a paramedic when I grow up."

She looked down at her purple knuckles, one looked fractured. Her lip still felt puffy. It was split on the inside. She'd always like to fight. But lately, it had meant something more. A release from the anger that had been building, a little escape of steam before the whole thing blew. Normally, it was at the bar, anonymous in her jeans and black t-shirt. But last night she made a mistake and let an idiot goad her in to a heap of trouble: a fist fight in uniform.

"So, I'm bad. I don't go to heaven. So, you can come over here."

He nodded.

"I'm sorry," she said, her elbows on her knees. "I'm sorry you're stuck with me, and I'm sorry that they left you alone." And in that moment her breath caught as she realized: *his mom had known this was coming.*

He looked at the sky as the air filled with sirens. "I always knew I wasn't good enough."

Molasses in Winter

At nine thirty at night, the very last thing Shea wanted to do was move her ass. It was cold and slippery out. She really wanted a glass of wine. The twins had been awful since they got home from school, and the baby was three. That seemed to be enough. Any time she told people he was three they went "oh!" and then winced. "The terrible threes!" "Yes, yes, it's true," she'd say, although she wasn't sure age had anything to do with it. The other two were eight and it wasn't the baby who wet toilet paper and stuck it to the ceiling like the world's biggest spit ball, or who squeezed an entire tube of toothpaste into the sink, or who stomped on a laundry pod just to see what it would do. She'd spent nearly the last decade of her life cleaning up after small people and keeping them alive. Which was why she looked like she did. Which was why, she reminded herself, she needed to move her ass.

She emerged from the bathroom, where she'd squeezed into her running tights and pulled her hair back to find Ed laying on their bed, shirtless, hands behind his head. "You're really going to leave me?"

It was tempting to crawl in next to him, to run her fingers through his chest hair, to hook her thigh over his hip and justify missing her run cause they got sweaty. She'd turn on her electric

117

blanket and cuddle in. They still had last week's John Oliver. But, the band of her sports bra was digging into her right rib something fierce; reminding her that this body was not the one that she wanted. "I'm gonna do a thousand miles this year."

"But the monsters?" He pointed out the door.

She laughed, "You made them."

"Aw shit," he said, sitting up and grabbing the remote. "Guess I'll have to make do with Sports Center."

"Let's not pretend you're unhappy about that." She bent over to lace up her shoes. Pressed her palms to the floor and felt the stretch through her whole body. *Yes, this was the right thing to do.*

"If you stayed, I would read with you. I have...a...book... around here somewhere," he searched his side table half-heartedly. "Or! Or, we could, you know talk?" He wiggled his eyebrows in a way that told her that he absolutely wasn't talking about talking.

"How would my ass get any smaller?"

"For the record, you are the only one who has anything negative to say about the size of your ass."

He was lying. Plenty of people, herself included, had a problem with the size of Shea's ass. One wouldn't think that it was anyone else's business, but just like when she was pregnant and the entire world felt entitled to touch her belly, now everyone felt the need to share their dieting or exercise tips, as if the size of one's body was the only indicator of health. If one more skinny bitch took something out of her cart at the grocery store, or one more dude-bro assumed it was her first time at the gym, she was gonna let the murder thoughts win. But Ed didn't know. He didn't live in a body that people were allowed to comment on, and Shea knew debating was the first step toward not getting her miles in tonight. She was going to use this anger as fuel.

"Well then," she said, "I'm going to go run my perfect ass around Flat Rock Park. I'll be home in an hour. Love you"

"Love you too! And good choice," he said. "The lighting there is good, and it's small and well patrolled."

Flat Rock Park was well lit, safe, and small. Also, the trail loop was less than a mile and it bored the shit out of Shea, and that's why she wasn't going there.

• • •

In second grade her teacher taught them about mass by having them weigh themselves in front of the other children, and write it on a big poster sized chart. She could still smell the orange marker. She weighed twice what the smallest girl in the class did. It was the first time she'd ever thought about bodies as something that could be too much. That she was too much.

• • •

Shea parked at the back of a seafood restaurant's a lot. It was better lit than the Okalawa Greenway's lot, and she had deniability. If one of Ed's work buddies saw her car, they wouldn't think anything of her at a restaurant, but at the trailhead was another story. She dug the headlamp Ed didn't know she had out of the glove compartment and strapped it on. She pulled her hood up and her gloves on. She beeped her car locked, hopped over a flower bed, and a small ditch, and then she was on the trail. Once she was away from cars, she tapped the Bluetooth earbud to start her music. *See Ed*, she thought, *I'm being safe. Staying aware of my surroundings.*

February in Western North Carolina. The woods were mostly bare branches and sticks, except for the rhododendron. The snakes that she had to be careful of in the summer were asleep underground. The New Year's Resolution runners were petering out. She hated what they did to the trails the first two weeks of the year. It would start raining in March and wouldn't stop until May, but right now, besides being a little bit chilly, it was perfect for trail running. No excuses. Nineties and early 2000's hip hop slammed into her ears. DMX. Ice Cube. Biggie. She hated every moment of running. She had to distract herself with beats from her clubbing days. Tunes that reminded her of shaking her less

119

substantial ass. She needed to let her mind wander, separate from her body, or else every step was torture. "But what about a runner's high?" Someone would ask. "That's after," she'd say. After she felt invincible. During though? During she wanted to die.

So it was that she wasn't paying attention to what she was doing, as she ran along the dark-wooded path. She couldn't hear her own footfalls on the asphalt trail, let alone anyone else's.

So, it wasn't the girl's screams that stopped her.

Or the glint of the gun.

It was the bright white of his bare ass that turned her head and the lamp. Even then it took a moment for her brain to switch from the Ruff Ryders anthem to what she was seeing. Four legs on the ground behind a garbage can. She had to kick the man very hard with her zero drop minimalist runners to get him off the girl. But she thought Ed would be proud of how she took charge and got control of the gun. The girl's eyes were huge as Shea pointed the gun at the man, the trigger guard tight to her gloved finger. "Go! Go!" She growled at the girl, unable to ascertain her volume with the earbuds in her ears. The man was huge, tall and muscular. There was no way that she could control him for long even with the gun. She didn't know what to do. *Should she try to bring him in? Hold the gun on him while she called 911?* Hot panic began to bubble up her throat, but it wasn't until he turned, and squinted into her headlamp that everything became real.

Fuck, she thought. *It had to be him.*

She couldn't do anything. She couldn't speak. She couldn't move. She told herself that he couldn't tell it was her. The light was in his eyes. She'd barely said a word. *Would he even recognize her anyway?* She waved the gun at him until he ran away. Then she sat down on the log and tried to make a plan. How could she turn him in, and stay safe herself?

● ● ●

The summer she got her period her family moved to a new town and she was so nervous about starting at a new school that she forgot to eat and her baby fat disappeared. No one noticed the eating, or the headaches, or her bloody cuticles, but everyone noticed she no longer had a double chin.

• • •

At home, she hid the gun somewhere Ed would never look, in her running gear drawer beneath the pile of high compression bras. She didn't have a plan. She was only trying to keep her breathing at a normal rate and her hands from shaking. She showered, and slipped into bed beside him. He molded his body against her curves, wrapped his arm around her waist and pulled her tight to him. "Glad you're home," he whispered, his mouth on her neck behind her ear.

"Me, too," she said, and for the first time allowed herself to think about how close she'd come to not. *What if he had seen her before she'd seen him? What if she'd been the first woman to that spot?* She was still thinking about a man with a gun in the woods, her woods, when Ed's phone went off. He had been sleeping deeply, and was clumsy and slow, and it took forever. She was sure he'd woken up the whole house.

"Well, shit," he said. "Alright," and hung up. "Got to go in," he said to Shea his voice thick with sleep, his breath sour, before he rolled out of bed and got dressed. "Love you," he said leaving the room. When his car started and his headlights flashed across the bedroom wall, she was reminded of that glowing white slice of ass in the dark, and she knew exactly why he'd been called in. She spent the rest of the night looking at the ceiling.

• • •

She got the twins to school, and the baby to preschool, locked and relocked all the doors and spent the morning trying to distract herself by cleaning things that probably hadn't been cleaned in the ten years they'd lived in that house. She pulled the TV stand and the dressers away from the wall and vacuumed behind them. She bleached the utensil tray. She flipped all the mattresses and remade the beds with fresh linen. She started cleaning her stove, so she was within earshot of the TV for the local news at noon. She knew there would be something, this was big, very big if the woman knew her attacker.

The reporter came on, polished in her blue suit and big blonde hair, and said all of the things that Shea expected to hear. *Last night. Okalawa Greenway. Small town. Interrupted sexual assault. Gun.*

And then the woman from the park came on, and Shea's breath caught. The wave of fear she'd felt last night came back in a cold rush. The woman still had the same wide eyes. She brushed her bangs out of her face with long, thin fingers. "I'm so very grateful to the person who saved me. I would love to meet you and thank you in person, and the police have just a few questions."

Oh, no. Shea thought.

Then the reporter was back, and Shea had to sit down, more unexpected words. *Unknown attacker. Witness wanted for questioning. Shit,* she thought. She couldn't be identified as a witness. Danger. Danger. Danger.

"Can you tell us anything about the witness?" asked the reporter.

Oh fuck, she thought.

"Rescuer," the victim said.

Shea's palms were sweaty and her heart was speeding. The fitness tracker on her wrist beeped a warning.

"Yes, rescuer."

"That's very important," said the woman whose face Shea would never be able to forget. "They aren't in trouble. I just didn't get a good look at the man who attacked me, but I think that they did."

Why does she keep saying they?

"Why is that?" asked the reporter.

"Because they were wearing headlamp," said the woman,

"Their light was in my eyes, so I couldn't see, but I assume they could."

"That's why you don't know if the rescuer was a man or a woman? You couldn't see."

"Right. I couldn't see their face and they only spoke one word and I was scared and…" She trailed off and started crying.

"Understandable," said the reporter. "What about their body?"

"They know who they are."

"Did you not see about how tall?"

"I already told this to the police. The witness knows. If they could just come forward, the police will protect their identity, they don't have to be afraid." *Oh fuck, oh fuck, oh fuck. No police.*

"Really, not even an outline, or a hair color? Black skin? White?"

The victim was pissed. "Listen, I told the police this already. They had a headlamp. I couldn't see their face. They had a hood over their head. I was laying on the ground so everyone would seem tall. They were dressed in dark clothes."

"But the body? Surely you could see a body shape? Men and women look very different.:

"They were fat okay. Like very, very fat. I couldn't tell if they were male or female cause of the fat."

"Oh," said the reporter, raising her eyebrows and holding her mouth in a stupid o shape. The victim just stared at the floor and ground her teeth together.

Shea's cheeks were hot.

The reporter cleared her throat, "If you know anything about this attack…"

But Shea wasn't listening. *Too verys? Really?*

• • •

Every holiday her grandmother would all but shovel food down her throat. Every gathering always included a meal where you weren't finished until you were uncomfortable and sleepy. And between events her mother would put them both on every diet imaginable. Cabbage soup. Weight Watchers. Intermittent fasting. No carbs.

Shea stopped wearing jeans and said that she liked the freedom of dresses, but really it was that she couldn't bear to see her mother's face in the doorway of a changing room as she asked for an even bigger size, again.

• • •

The house felt tight. Suffocating. She put on her running clothes, and drove to Okalawa in a confusing route to try to throw off anyone tailing her. If he'd recognized her he'd never expect her to be here. It was busy. That was good. Much busier than it normally was. Much busier than it should be… Considering. Moving her legs felt good though. She felt like she'd been holding her breath since the night before, it felt amazing to fill her lungs with air and focus on the rhythm of her steps and her breathing. And when she came to the fork in the trail where she had to decide if she was going to go back to the scene of the crime, she did. The yellow caution tape made a twenty-foot circle around the garbage can. For the first time she wondered, *why here? A trail in the woods? Next to a smelly garbage can? And he was an attractive guy.* "Stop," she told herself. She knew it wasn't about getting laid. It wasn't about sex. It was about power. Pain. Violence. Destruction. It didn't matter that he was sexy and had lots of partners. It didn't matter what the victim looked like either.

"Excuse me, ma'am?"

She looked toward the voice. It came from a man in a uniform on the other side of the trail. *Shit*, she thought, but smiled, and climbed out of the ditch. "Hi Billy," she said. "Nice to see you again." He didn't recognize her. "It's Shea Alexander," she said her last name real slow. "I changed my hair," she said although she hadn't.

"Oh, I thought that was you. Ed tell you what happened here?"

"No," she said, shaking her head.

His brows came together, "Oh," he said. "I just figured that's why you were here."

"I like to run," she said. "I saw the news, and I guess my curiosity got the better of me."

"I didn't know you were a runner! Hard on the knees, isn't it? Good thing you weren't here last night!"

"Yes," Shea near about shouted. "Night running can be dangerous."

"And you can't count on a guy coming out of the woods to save you, that's for sure."

"It was a man? The rescuer? I didn't realize anyone had come forward." She had to hold her face very still to keep from smiling.

"Not that I've heard," he said. "But must be a man, based on the description."

Shea said, "Well better get a move on. I need to go get my kids," grinding her teeth as she jogged away, quicker than usual. She wanted him to see there was nothing wrong with her fucking knees.

• • •

When Ed slid the too small engagement ring on her finger she knew she needed to do something. "I'll get it fixed," he said, his cheeks red.

"No," she said. "I was going to lose some weight. I am going to lose some weight. This will be a good motivator."

And so she didn't eat anything white, no flour, sugar, or potatoes for a year and she walked down the aisle thinner than she'd ever been. Three months after, they sat on the couch eating pizza together and joking, and she thought she'd never been so happy. Until on a commercial Ed turned and said: "You know I'm concerned you're gaining weight," wiped sauce off his chin and took another piece of pizza, and she excused herself to the bathroom where she threw up and cried.

• • •

Ed was home, and sitting at the kitchen table eating a turkey sandwich when she got there with the kids. "I would have made you something hot," she said, piling the backpacks on the counter.

"I know," he said. "But I was starving."

"I was going to do meatloaf." She took out their lunch boxes and put their sandwich containers and water bottles in the dishwasher.

"You still can." He ate in big thoughtless bites.

"You won't be hungry at dinner."

"Just wrap mine up. It's better the next day anyway."

"Are you on the park attack?" She had permission slips in front of her and she didn't look up as she asked. She couldn't look that interested; he was good at his job.

"You know I can't..." He looked at her and shook his head. "All I could think about was how happy I was that you were at Flat Rock last night."

"Has the rescuer come forward?"

"Not yet."

"But they will?"

"Probably, it's a small town. Unless they have something to hide. Warrants, or are undocumented or something." He put the last bite in his mouth and brushed the crumbs from his chin.

"You don't know anything though? There's no camera in the parking lot?"

"Here? And this tiny town no. Too many people think that's an invasion of their privacy. But a couple more of these attacks and they'll change their minds." He took a bite and chewed. "I wish we had the gun though. She says the rescuer wrestled the gun away from the attacker. That let her escape. She doesn't know what happened next or who has the gun now. The victim says he pressed the gun to her head though. There would be DNA."

"Isn't there…... A kit?"

"Do you know how long it takes to get a rape kit processed? She is better chance of winning the lottery than finding this bastard."

"You haven't found the gun? In the woods at Okalawa?"

"If it is, we haven't found it yet. But Jason's leading that search again tomorrow when it's light."

She couldn't help herself. "Do you think maybe the victim's description of the rescuer could be wrong?" She wiped the counter and put his plate in the dishwasher.

"She's pretty adamant."

"Do you think maybe the description will keep the rescuer from coming forward?"

Ed scratched his head. "I don't think men care that much about being called fat. But that's a fair point. I'll ask the media to maybe change how they frame that, yeah? Big, maybe? Could mean muscular, too. I'll ask her about that a bit more. Maybe the rescuer is one of these no neck gym guys."

"What does Jason think? He's a big guy."

"He hasn't been in on the interview. He says he's too busy working the park."

Ed opened the cupboard where Shea stashed all the kids' unhealthy snacks, and pulled out a bag of goldfish crackers and stuck his hand inside. "I'm going to make meatloaf! Stop ruining your dinner," she said.

"I'll eat it. I'm going to go take a nap. I got to go back in later. Check out the phone lines and see if any tips of come in. Then go back to the scene, I want to see it at the time of day that it happened, you know?"

"I need to run before you go. So go nap."

He took a deep breath, and she could tell he wanted to fight about it. About her staying home. About her staying safe.

"Until you get that treadmill fixed, I got to run outside. You want me to make a pie? Those apples are going."

"I never say no to pie," he said climbing the stairs.

• • •

If one more doctor told her that pregnancy was a good time to lose weight, she was going to lose it. If one more nurse looked at her with disgust. If one more random old lady at the grocery store asked her the due date and then with wide eyes made a comment about how she must be having multiples. If she ever heard the word huge to describe her body ever again, she was going to murder someone.

. . .

Ed was scooping a second ball a vanilla ice cream onto his cereal bowl of pie when she came down the stairs in her gear, carrying her hoodie.

"I wish you wouldn't go," he said, his mouth full.

"I wish I could eat dessert without it going directly to my ass."

"I like it," he said, sliding his hands over her hips, cupping her ass and squeezing. "I do like these pants though."

"I know," she said. But couldn't tell him what it was like to live in a body that most people thought was too big. What it felt like to always be trying to make herself smaller, lighter, less. Running was magical. It both reduced the size of her body, and made her feel strong, valuable and worthy. And tonight, she needed to run for a couple of reasons.

She got in the car and drove to the seafood restaurant, but carried her headlamp in her hand into the park. She didn't want to draw attention to herself. She put the hoodie on. Jogged down the path, past the caution tape and to the little creek that ran through the park. The gun was heavy in her pocket. She planned to find a spot near the creek to hide it. Maybe wedged next to a rock at the water's edge, or trapped against a log. She knew that the DNA was important, so she hoped that there was some left after she'd wiped all of the areas that she had touched. She couldn't come forward. Couldn't put herself or her family in danger like that. But she also couldn't let him get away with this. So she searched the bank for the perfect spot.

"Did you hide the gun here?" Jason said from behind her. He'd moved silently. She jumped at the sound, her hand finding the grip of the gun in her pocket. "I searched but didn't find it. But Ed already told you that."

"I didn't tell him anything."

"Only because you don't want him to know that you were here, that you lied. Don't pretend you're protecting me"

"I didn't rape anyone."

"I'm guessing too, you don't much like how the witness describes you, and that's why you haven't come forward."

Shea blushed at how easily he understood. How obvious she was to him. "I didn't think you would know it was me."

"You didn't think I'd recognize you?"

She nodded. "In the five years you've been Ed's partner, you've never had a conversation with just me. You pretend I'm not in the room. No matter what I do, I'm invisible.

"I'm a detective, I don't have to like you to notice you." He took a step towards her. She stepped back, but the bank was slick and rocky, she had nowhere to go.

Before she knew what was happening, he'd knocked her to her back, and all the air had left her lungs. He was pushing her into the creek, her hair was wet, it was only inches before her head would be under the water.

"You're a detective!" She wheezed.

"Yes, and look at this body I discovered in the park. Must be a second attack. Maybe a copycat!"

Memories flooded her. Jason in her backyard kicking a soccer ball with the twins while Ed manned the grill. Jason sitting on her couch with a beer in his hand, the football game on the TV. Eating her Christmas cookies, and coolly thanking her for the lasagna she'd dropped at his house when his mother died. *Had he always hated her?*

"This will kill him. It's not just about me, this will end him."

"Better him than me though, yeah?" He said with one last push, right before her head went under the water. Her mouth filled with gritty water, and what she hoped was leaves and twigs brushed her cheeks and forehead. She thought about how Ed would starve to death without her. About how her children would go to school smelly, and they would all forget about her because they were too little. She needed more time.

But then she remembered what was in her pocket, and she pulled the trigger.

The pistol recoiled against her belly, but instead of a steam-roller trying to crush her, Jason became dead weight. She used her hips to throw him off, and pulled herself out of the water. She pushed him in, and looked around for footprints, shuffled them useless. Then she ran a half mile down the trail and threw the gun in the deepest part of the river.

• • •

She puked when she crossed the finish line, but she still crossed it. A fucking half marathon. Miles and miles of training. Freezing cold mornings. Fish when she wanted burgers. Kale when she wanted fries. Sunburn. Chafed everything. It was hard, but she did it anyway. Ed slipped his arm under hers to support her rub-ber legs. Her mom and kids held signs. No one commented on how most other people had already left. She'd been last. It didn't matter. She could barely move and her heels were bleeding, but she finished.

On the way to the car Jason jogged up. "I forgot what time it started! And I thought I missed it. They were taking down tables and the podiums and stuff and I had to... wait, you were still running? They took it all down while you were still running? What's your time?"

She shrugged. "Molasses in winter," she said and then let her family take her out for ice cream to celebrate, but she couldn't taste it, and she threw up when they got home.

• • •

On the way home she tried to justify what she'd done. He'd deserved it. Or, it was self-defense. But a trap door in the back of her mind opened over a pit of guilt. She could have stopped this earlier, gone to the police with what she knew. *No one had to die.* Had it been the victim's description? Or implicating her husband's best friend and partner? She knew well enough not to look at that question too closely. Ed was going to be devastated, she needed to keep it together for him.

When she got home, she put all her clothes, and her favorite shoes in a garbage bag and stuffed it in the bottom of her closet to get rid of when Ed wasn't home. She got in the shower before he had a chance to notice her soaking wet hair.

"What happened to your belly?" Ed said, his head peeking through the curtain.

"I fell. Tripped over a branch at Flat Rock."

"You gotta be more careful out there, baby. There's fucking danger everywhere."

"I will love," she said, and pulled him in with her, fully clothed.

Hell, or High Water

On the third day of the April rains, he left to check the fish mill. "That bitch," as he called the river, was swollen and feisty with the flood. Left alone she'd burst the dams. He was not prone to sentimentality, but Kate could tell by the way he paused at the door he didn't want to leave. He never left her alone. In the last four years she hadn't slept without his arm over her torso. He lurked outside when her bowel movements kept her in the outhouse longer than usual. She didn't bathe by herself.

But by day nine, Kate feared the bitch had taken him.

She'd have to wait until the waters receded to be sure. Lord willing. If the French Broad River had seen fit to carry him out of Henderson County she'd never know. Roy didn't carry identification, those hunter's orange suspenders were good enough anywhere in the county, but Tennessee would be different. He might even make it to the Mississippi. Roy would be livid to have his bones rest anywhere other than here - the county he'd never left. But Kate thought there was something romantic about his body becoming part of the water. She imagined he'd get to touch the ocean. But she didn't have time for imagining; there was too much to be done.

A cottage in the woods conjured quixotic visions of snuggling in heirloom quilts, sipping cocoa next roaring fires or idealistic notions of off-grid homesteading, organic gardens and frolicking wildlife. The cabin Kate shared with Roy was more hunt camp than bed and breakfast. It was cold and dark in January, hot and dark in July. A day didn't pass where she didn't trap or shoo something that slithered or squeaked from a hidden corner. The rot riddled roof was little more than the final obstacle for the water to find its way around before it dripped off the ceiling beam and down the back of Kate's neck. She'd made a tent over the baby's bed with an old blanket. As the tent saturated, she switched it for a different one. The water didn't evaporate this time of year. Soon she'd run out of anything close to dry.

She'd kept the fire going. It was harder done than said. It was Roy's job to bring in the wood and let it dry from sodden to merely damp inside the house. On his last day he hadn't. Feeding the sopping logs she dragged inside to the hungry flames, filled the cabin with smoke. She'd had no other choice. The fire was as ravenous for fuel as she was, as greedy as the baby for her attention, and as stingy with comfort as Roy, only occasionally providing her with a moment of warmth. Kate wouldn't have described them as one of those couples who were just co-existing, but his absence showed her all the ways that she'd come to rely more on his labor and less on his company.

Roy was a quiet man. She wasn't privy to his thoughts or plans, but she was surprised when she looked in the cupboard to find it so bare. She couldn't remember the last time he went for supplies, but would have sworn that there had been extra oatmeal, and shortening, and at least one more bag of milk powder. The rain did that to a person though; made you think thoughts that weren't your own. Sometimes, the roar of the water falling from heaven made it impossible to have any thoughts at all.

On the tenth day, despite hanging, all of the blankets were soaked, the towels and the flour sacks too. Everything smelled of must, sour and smoke. Kate decided that Roy would have to forgive her if she used his extra shirt to keep the drips off the baby. Crossing to the bedroom portion of their one-room cabin, she paused. He might not mind her borrowing the shirt, but he would hate her going in his trunk. It wasn't only his thoughts he kept private from Kate. In the four years they'd shared that cabin, she'd never looked in the foot locker before. Army issue, from when his dad fought the gooks. It didn't have a lock but the memory of his hand across her cheekbone was enough.

As she stood in front of the battered green box, her hand moved to her face. The pad of her thumb traced the scar on her bottom lip, fingers pinching the always tender bridge of her nose. Her muscles remembered fighting his hands for air as he squeezed her throat. Her eyes saw stars, again. A phantom of pain burned under her skin. The baby's cry in the other room startled her. She closed her eyes and lifted the latch, opening them to find the trunk empty. Her breath caught in her throat. Disbelief struck her dumb; she blinked, and rubbed her eyes. She thought of catching a deer in the headlights of her father's car. Then the black snake of doubt that she'd kept coiled in the back of her mind slithered out and she fell to her knees on the wood floor, planks swollen with damp, and she knew.

• • •

Kate never imagined a life in the woods. When she'd first seen Roy looking up at her riding the Ferris wheel at the Mountain Fair, in autumn of her senior year, she'd been contemplating her escape from under her parent's thumbs. He was big, dark haired and square jawed. Standing with his hands in his pockets, his eyes never left her. Some of the girls in her class, the brainy and the beautiful ones, talked about escaping to university or to the city. Kate just wanted her own money and for her mother to stop hassling her about her back brace. The bend in her spine that made her stand with her hip out limited her dating life enough without the coordinating magnetic accessories. She'd wondered, in one of the many quiet moments in the expanse of time between that moment on the Ferris wheel and this one in the cabin, if the brace that had driven so many suitors away had been a draw for Roy. He couldn't take his eyes off her. Close up, Roy was older than she'd hoped, but the intensity of his gaze thrilled her. She'd intentionally walked behind the goat barn, the quiet darkness perfect for a first meeting. She'd never expected it would lead to this.

• • •

She ran her hand over the bottom of the trunk, her fingernails pulling at the edges, digging in the cracks. She scavenged the cabin fingering all his remaining things, finding them flimsy with abandonment. Rocking the baby next to the skimpy fire she poured over the morning he left. Their relationship was fraught with moments, days and weeks even, of miscommunication; times when she had no idea what he wanted. Times when he chose to tell her with his fist instead of his mouth.

The events of that morning seven days ago were still at the front of her mind as she re-buttoned the front of her blouse and placed the baby back in his bed. She found a box and made a place for him under the kitchen table. The labor provided her a respite from her thoughts so she busied herself with tasks that taxed her body. Somewhere between priming the well pump and hauling the heavy pails of water into the kitchen for boiling, she realized that it wasn't only the morning he left she should be examining. He had planned this. She pulled up her long skirt and peered at the calloused flesh encircling her right ankle.

• • •

When he'd first brought her to the cabin, she'd thought it had all been a misunderstanding. She was the one that said "let's go somewhere more private," while he pressed her into the back of the goat barn and kissed her neck. The ride up the mountain under his arm made her pulse pound. Her friends were going to be so jealous. Even as he stripped her clothes, removed her earrings and broke off the pendant her parents had given her, it wasn't fear that dominated her thoughts, but confusion. This wasn't at all like the love scenes she'd seen on TV. It wasn't until he closed the metal cuff around her ankle, and locked it to a chain attached to the bed, that fear came. Slow and cold, it filled her chest and weakened her joints, her heart beating like the wings of a hummingbird at her mother's feeder. She'd beaten herself up for years since, laying in the dark staring at the log beam above her head, his thick arm across her chest. The weight of the chain trapping her in the night took years to learn to ignore.

He'd finally unlocked the cuff when pregnancy swelling turned her foot purple and her toenails blue. "I reckon you can't run regardless," he'd said, placing the cuff on the mantel. That was three months ago. He hadn't touched her in that time either. Kate found her mind spinning the same circles as it had her first year at the cabin. Nothing made sense.

As she lay in bed looking up at the beam, she felt too light without the weight of his arm. It was too quiet without his snores. He was gone. She was free. She took a deep breath and allowed a smile to peck at her lips. She was free. Then the horror of the situation revealed itself. She was free, except she was starving, and had been for days. She was free, but her cabin was waterlogged, falling down and unfit to live in. She was free, but she had a newborn and no earthly idea where she was, or where she could go.

• • •

In the beginning he'd brought her wildflower roots and seeds to plant around the cabin. He'd rubbed her sore ankle and applied a salve when her skin was raw. He'd brought her treats from the store when he went in for supplies. He was often gentle in the dark. If she could ignore the cuff and his waiting outside the outhouse while she shat, she could pretend it was a relationship. And now he was gone. If she didn't leave soon, she'd be gone too.

She put on her winter skirt and blouse and strapped the baby to her front. Her shawl fashioned a sling with only minor tailoring. She wrapped her feet in rags; Roy had thrown away everything from her former life, and worn his only pair of boots when he left. Even if she had things to take, she wouldn't. This could be a test.

He'd tested her before. The second spring, he'd taken her chains off and they'd gone down to the river. He'd stripped naked and waded, washing the winter off his body in the bracing water. She'd waited at the bank. Watched him move further from shore. Calculated the distance and the time it would take him to get back to the bank. Casually looked over her shoulder at the density of the woods and wondered how far she could get before he even noticed she was gone. But she wasn't watching closely enough. She didn't make it to the rhododendron before his meaty hand squeezed her upper arm. Without a mirror she didn't know the damage that was done to her face, but her body was black with bruises. Her chains felt tighter for months.

He would test her. Now that the baby was a couple months old, he would watch from the woods. Now that she was almost on her feet again. It was a trick. She was almost sure. Fear penetrated, lingered, like the smoke in her clothes.

• • •

She arranged the house so it looked like they were coming back. Leaving her collection of heart shaped stones on the windowsill made her chest ache, but he would never expect her to abandon them. The rain wasn't as loud on the roof as it had been yesterday. She looked down at her baby's smooth brow and knew it had to be now. She slipped out the front door and pulled it closed behind her with shaking hands. The rags felt strange beneath her feet, but her toes had not forgotten the way to the gate. When she was heavily pregnant, he'd allowed her to walk the gate path, back and forth, to encourage the baby to come. Then, she'd touched the padlock that held the halves of the barbed wire gate together with each pass, willing the next time for it to be open. Today she'd brought the axe.

The moss beneath her feet squished as she hurried toward

the gate. A drop of rain slid off her nose and dripped onto her upper lip. Would he be sitting just on the other side of the gate? How far would he let them go before she felt his hand on her arm, squeezing. Would she survive this time? If so, what would she lose? Her teeth? A finger? The ability to breathe through her nose? The ability to walk? How many months would she wear his marks? Or would it be years? The gate was just around the bend. Everything in her said turn around. To wait him out. But she pressed on. It wasn't much of a choice really, she thought, the gate coming within view. *She'd die either way.*

When she saw it, she dropped the axe and ran. The baby's head hit her in the larynx with each step. She gasped and choked, but didn't stop. She hugged tighter, pressing the baby's weight to her chest, half in an attempt to breathe and half the need to cling to something solid as everything she knew shifted. She stopped just short of the swinging gate. She watched the water form a stream in the beaten path, a river running away from their cabin. She stepped outside the gate, held her breath, and listened for the sound of his boots in the wet moss, or the grind of his teeth, but only heard birdsong, and her own blood crashing through her veins, and she knew he was exactly this cruel.

Porch Light Salvation

The mother stood over a steaming pot, stirring, as the little girl came in and stared at her toes.

"Mason pushed me," the little girl said, tucking a dark curl behind her ear.

"Are you okay?" her mother asked, watching the minute hand sweep the face of the clock. Her toes tapped on the worn linoleum.

"I scraped my knee... and I ripped my pants. I'm sorry, I didn't mean to." The girl wouldn't look up.

The mother tried not to show her annoyance. More demands on her limited resources, the need to try to fix the pants, the inevitable need to ask him for money to buy new ones. She could feel his fingertips pressing into the tender flesh on the back of her arm as he asked why she needed more money. Ten years of running circles to keep him happy had worn her thin.

"We'll look at your knee in the tub. Please put away your crayons, wash your hands, and set the table."

The little girl carefully collected her crayons and carried her picture to the fridge.

"Can you get me the crab magnet, Mama. It's too high."

The mother leaned over the sink and peered out the window into the darkness that hid the driveway before going over to help. Seeing the crab holding another piece of crayon art, she rearranged the magnets to free the crab and placed it in her daughter's tiny hand, her own shaking as she did.

"I always want the crab one, don't I, Mama?" the little one said affixing her picture to the fridge, but her mother had already moved on to something else. Stepping back, the girl appraised her work and pushed her picture higher, knocking papers and magnets to the floor in her attempt. Scrambling to pick up the papers, her eyes wide and breathing erratic, she only made the mess larger.

The crash pulled the mother's attention from the twenty other things she was trying to do in preparation for his arrival.

"Emma, baby, you need to set the table."

"I'm sorry, Mama." Tears welled in her large green eyes.

The mother dropped to her knees and gathered the scattered papers and the tiny girl into her arms. The mother could feel her pulse in her temple. " Set the table, now. He'll be home soon."

The girl skipped to the utensil drawer. The mother gathered the pile of fallen bills and past due notices and tucked them away, thought it was better to hide them anyway. She didn't want to remind him of their debt.

The mother returned to the stove and added some more garlic powder, more salt and pepper. No matter what she did, he would hate it, but she had to try. Peering out the window again, snowflakes were starting to fall. A cold front moved in that afternoon, making the drafty house colder than usual.

The stew was finished. The clock said ten after six. She'd made it with five minutes to spare. Finishing with a flourish Emma said "Tah dah!" smiling at her mother, gaps where her front teeth used to be. Her eyes widened. "Oh no! I forgot to wash my hands!"

"I won't tell if you won't. Go wash them now, and then get to the table to wait for Daddy."

The mother heard the thump, thump of tiny heels trotting down the hall, followed by the sound of running water and

Emma singing her ABC's. Straightening the table setting, she looked out the window again. The night was black, the snow clouds blocking the moon. The porch light had been broken for days but he hadn't taken the time to fix it. He liked that it trapped her inside. Up on this mountain, with no neighbors and no streetlights. Dinner was ready, the table was set, she'd open his beer when she saw headlights, but not before.

"What's for dinner, Mama?" she asked, sitting down. Ankles crossed, hands in her lap, like always.

"Beef stew, baby."

"With onions?"

"Yes, of course with onions. Your Daddy likes 'em," the mother watched her small daughter's mouth turn down. "I'll try not to give you any. But you have to clean your plate."

"I know, Mama. There are children in Africa…I know."

The mother kept one eye on the window and one on her daughter's animated conversation about the class guinea pig. She wiped the counter again. Minutes passed. The house was spotless. She was in her best house dress, not fancy enough that he would think she'd had company, but nice enough that he'd like what he saw. She'd done her hair, leaving it down like he liked it. She didn't often wear it loose, having learned quickly that it hurt less when he yanked it if it was in a braid.

More minutes passed. She sat kiddy corner to Emma. It felt weird to be sitting, but he was late. Late meant one of two things, his supervisor held him back and he'd be pissed and charge in like a bull after a red cape. He would flail and rage and she and Emma needed to stay out of the way. Or he was drinking with his friends, and he'd be happy and loud, but simmering just beneath the surface was a well of suspicion and cruelty. Drunk was scarier because they couldn't run. Their avoidance only made him meaner.

"I'm hungry, Mama."

The little girl's words startled her awake. She hadn't slept at all the night before and had fallen asleep at the table. Afraid, her eyes darted to the clock. He was over an hour late.

"I'm so hungry."

The mother looked at the pot on the stove. There was no need for Emma to eat it if he wasn't going to be there. He would ask her if Emma ate the stew for dinner too, and screw it, she would look into his eyes and say yes.

She grabbed a plate to make a cheese sandwich. She watched as the plate shook in her trembling hands and she knew he would know. He could always tell when she was lying to him. He would wonder why Emma hadn't eaten the stew. He would ask why she was different, and why she got a special meal while he ate the slop. He would ask her if she thought he was a pig, and that was why she fed him the seconds. She imagined him throwing the scalding pot of stew at her, the brilliant heat, the blisters that would rise, the story she would make up about a tea kettle.

Looking at her daughter, she put the plate on the counter and collected the bread and cheese. She cut the sandwich into four tiny triangles. Emma squealed before she stuffed it in her face.

"Okay, baby, get your jammies on."

"But it's bath night."

"Not tonight, love. I can't bathe you and wait for Daddy to come home."

"But my knee!"

"Go get a nightie on, I'll get the first-aid kit and meet you in your bedroom."

She tidied the already spotless kitchen in case he came home while she was putting Emma to bed. The stew was simmering, she had a few minutes.

She found Emma in her pajamas sitting on the edge of her bed. Her bare knee red and raw.

"Where are your pants?"

Emma wouldn't meet her eyes. She got up and looked in the back of the girl's closet, where she often found things the little one didn't want her to see. Tiny pink leggings with a ripped and bloodied knee were wadded on the floor. She cleaned and bandaged the girl's leg, and then wrapped Emma in her arms.

"What happened with Mason?"

"We were playing tag and he pushed me onto the ground."

"On purpose? Did he apologize?"

"He didn't. He just called me a baby and ran away."

"Well, that's silly. You're not a baby."

"Addie says that he's only mean to me because he likes me. That's what boys do if they want to be your boyfriend."

She stroked the girl's soft tendrils and remembered the day the doctor pulled the baby screaming from between her legs. The happiest day of her life.

"If people, boys included, like you, they don't hurt you. They try to save you from pain. They'll do anything to protect you."

"But Daddy hurts you sometimes."

The mother kissed the girl and pulled her closer before she could see the wetness on her mother's face.

"Go to sleep, sweetheart. Remember if you hear yelling, stay in here," she whispered, unable to fill her lungs.

"I know, but Mama, we need to say prayers!"

She allowed the little girl to lead her in the Lord's prayer with the addition of a couple of extra verses about stuffed animals and candy. Nerves wound tighter with every minute that passed.

"Mommy, you didn't ask me what I'm supposed to do if I ever find you sleeping and you won't wake up?"

"Oh…right," the mother said, distracted, listening for his truck in the driveway.

"I remember it! I go to the phone and press 9-1-1 and tell them to come to 35 Windy Way. That's where we live. Then I go to the front window and watch for the lights."

"Smart girl! Just try to sleep, okay? I love you. I love you, so, so much."

The daughter's breathing became slow and even. Her mother longed to stay in that warm safe bed. But she knew what would happen if he found her there, and his dinner not on the table.

She left the room, peering as long as she dared through the slit between the door and the jamb. Treasuring every moment of her daughter's peace. This was it; he would be home soon.

She quickly washed her face, checked again that the house was perfect, stirred the stew and waited. Shortly after midnight headlights shone through the window. He parked crooked across the driveway, almost losing the front tires in the ditch. He was drunk. She ran to close Emma's bedroom door. Grabbing a beer from the fridge she opened it and braced herself. Ten years of fear had turned her into a caged animal. Always waiting for the next blow, physical senses sharp for self-preservation. Emotions dulled for the same reason.

It took a long time for the truck to turn off, and even longer to hear the driver's door shut. She waited, breath rigid in her chest. The bottom porch step creaked with the pressure of his two hundred plus pounds, and then a house-shaking boom filled the night before a profound silence rippled across.

She was wound so tight that it took more than a moment to realize what had happened.

He'd slipped on the step in the dark.

The porch light!

Her head felt like a balloon whose knot had come loose. Her thoughts bouncing and flapping all over, unable to stop, unable to rest, frantic, until finally they settled, spent and lifeless.

He would be angry.

She waited in fear but nothing happened. One breathless minute turned into five. She couldn't see out the window and didn't dare open the door.

Paralyzed, she watched the thermometer dip lower. It was freezing out there. She should go out there and help him. He was injured, but he could still hurt her. He might even be unconscious right now, but when he woke, this would somehow be all her fault. No one could survive the night outside in this weather. She needed to do something.

She put her fingers on the doorknob, but then saw the hand

shaped bruise around her wrist, and thought of the all of the others under her dress, of the cigarette burns on her inner thighs, and the bruise she found on Emma's arm yesterday that was a perfect match for her own. That angry purple mark on that tiny perfect arm screamed at her to stop. Wait. Listen.

Still nothing.

The thermometer showed well below freezing. Plug in your truck weather. The snow fell faster, white drifts filling the mullions of the windows. She could save him if she wanted to. Did she want to? When was the last time she did something because she wanted to? She was a terrible person for even considering this. She could open the door and drag him inside. She could call the ambulance and keep him warm while they navigated the snowy roads. Her heart banged against the inside of her ribs. She fisted her shaking hands; she knew what she wanted.

His favorite remark was to tell her how lazy she was. Dinner was disgusting, the bathroom was dirty, his clothes were laundered, mended or pressed incorrectly, she was ugly or fat or frigid, all because she was lazy. Their daughter's grades were bad not because she lived in fear, but because she was learning her mother's laziness. Didn't she know anything? Didn't she have respect for herself? Didn't she care that their house was a pig sty? Why was she so goddamned lazy?

Sinking to the floor, her back to the door, she told herself that her legs wouldn't carry, but they could. She was good at lying to herself. This was her chance. A smile crept across her lips as she realized that this time, she would be lazy.

Hours passed with no noise but the sound of blood rushing in her ears. She expected to feel terrible, but each moment of snowy silence settled her. Coming to the realization that he wasn't coming home, ever, the fear evaporated. She didn't have to wait on eggshells. She was done. She could go to bed. Before she could sleep, she had to know.

She stood and opened the door. Peering out into the night, the light from the hallway shone past her, down the steps and onto his snow-covered face. A gasp burst through her lips. In bare feet, she stepped out into the snow. Creeping as near as she dared, she held her fingers in front of his mouth, feeling nothing, she pressed them to his neck. His skin was clammy and cold. Dashing back into the house, she closed the door and caught herself on the wall.

This couldn't be real. She was dreaming, she'd fallen asleep at the table again. She pinched herself on the bicep, hard. Nothing but pain. Looking out through the window in the door she could see fat flakes of snow reflecting in the light from the hall and nothing but black beyond. But he was out there, and he was dead.

Slowly, wobbling like a sailor aboard his first ship, she went back to the kitchen. She turned off the stove and the lights. She opened the drawer and threw the bills on the floor. She stood in front of the open fridge and drank a beer straight from the bottle. This was her kitchen now. Dizzy with relief, she stumbled to Emma's room and crawled into bed, fully clothed. She shivered as she cuddled against her daughter, toes tingling, but her body light.

Frogs in a Pot

I need your eyes," Ben said, scanning the road through the windshield. "You're supposed to be the navigator and you're not paying attention." And then, under his breath, "like usual."

In fairness, she wasn't. Amanda was watching a huge group of blackbirds alight from an electrical line, together, a living swirl of beaks and feathers, rapid heartbeats and beady eyes; all moving as one. Oh, to have that intimacy, that instinctual familiarity; to know in their muscles and bones, to not even have to think to be so perfectly synched. There was a word for it, she knew, but it didn't come.

"Sorry," she said and looked at her phone. She was given the job of navigating so that she couldn't daydream, couldn't use this time to work either, "it's not for another mile." She reached over and turned on the radio to cover the uncomfortable silence.

When the voice came on, the reporter only said five words before Ben jabbed the button violently. "Not this shit again."

• • •

First it was just on the TV. A sideways glance from the newscaster as he read the teleprompter. A small tremble of the anchor's hand on the desk. Catastrophe at a distance. Not here. Everything so very far away. Fuzzy. Indistinct. They didn't know anyone affected. Maybe it wasn't as bad as all that? The Whitehouse issued loud declarations that everything was fine. Reports otherwise were lies they said, but it was creeping. Airports felt like bullseyes.

"Just follow these new rules," the President said. "For your protection."

Ben shook his head and rolled his eyes every time the talk of the changes came on the news, yet, he still bought months' worth of meat and a new freezer. He filled the pantry with fruit leather and boxed mac and cheese. There was a wall of toilet paper in their garage. "What's the harm?" he said, "just as long as we're together." Amanda stopped shoe shopping since there was nowhere to go. When she lost her job, no one takes pottery classes in a pandemic, she stopped sleeping and instead wandered the dark house, checking and rechecking their small daughter's room. "Don't worry," Ben said. "I'll take care of you." A police cruiser drove past their house every 30 minutes; it didn't make her feel any better.

• • •

The new normal meant no more daycare. Instead of spending her days encouraging students to mold mud into art, or attending gallery openings, or holed up in her studio, Amanda sat on her back deck, worked on her tan while she watched Violet splash in the sprinkler, and talked across the fence with her neighbor. Like Ben, Michael was now working from home due to the new government rules; unlike Ben, he wasn't holed up in the basement. Amanda was so grateful for his company, that when his wife came home from her job at the hospital each night, and he nodded goodbye, that she found herself pinching her nose and looking to the sky. She hadn't left the yard for weeks, and Ben progressively went to work earlier, and came back upstairs later. The first week she realized it didn't matter if it was five or not before she uncorked her wine, and now, she was lucky to make it past lunch. In bed at night, Amanda would tell Ben what Michael's wife saw at the hospital.

"Shh," he said. "We're safe. We're together. Michael isn't good for your mental health." She clenched her teeth, and held her breath until she saw stars behind her closed eyelids.

"I really like this though," he said, squeezing the new soft of her inner thigh, or the extra curve of her breast. "Sexy. Staying home suits you."

Soon, the windows in their neighbors' houses started going dark. She waited on the back deck for Michael all day, but he didn't show. The hollow in her chest widened. "I think people are leaving," she said that night over pot roast. "I think we should go, too."

"They're just afraid," he said, with a sneer, like fear was a weakness.

Sitting on the couch later, watching reruns, she asked him what was the first thing he was going to do when this was over. "I'm just going to be sad," he said. "I like this. I like us all being together. I like you being home. I like knowing where you are." And at his words she missed her students and her friends with a ferocity that gave her indigestion, and she hid the bags that she'd packed in the back of the closet.

The next night, she saw lights outside, and managed to make it to the driveway in time to see the Ramirezes from across the way turn the corner. Their Honda was filled to bursting and the tailgate bounced. When she woke Ben he said, "we're not like them." Amanda bit her tongue and squeezed her fingers into fists until her fingernails left blood in her palms. When the news started talking about thugs and gangsters, about perverts and pedophiles running to the woods to escape the police, she added weapons to her hidden bags and started YouTubing homesteading skills.

In the morning she hauled her body, stiff with insomnia, from her bed and into the kitchen. He was freshly showered, at the table, sipping coffee and scrolling his phone, waiting. She made his eggs and toast and the plate made a louder than usual smack as she laid them on the table. She winced.

"I feel like you don't want me here," he said.

"At the table? You wanna eat breakfast at your desk, too?"

"I would have thought that you would have been happy to spend more time with me, more time together."

"More time together? You're locked in your office all day. I've never been so lonely. You're close enough to supervise, to pop in and tell me I've left the clothes in the washer too long, but if I actually need you..."

"You don't feel safer with me home with everything that is going on out there?"

"You finally agree that something is going on? Can we please, can we please get out of here. I can pack us up, and we can get in the car, and take Violet and just—"

"You, think we are in danger. You, are afraid and anxious. Don't I make you feel better?"

Amanda bit the cuticle on her index finger.

"You are my everything. Have I ever given you any reason not to trust me?" he said. He hadn't, she thought, before.

• • •

When the men in uniforms came to the door, she was too afraid to feel smug. She was too busy trying to still her hands and her heart as the men explained that their house now belonged to the government, and they would have to pay a tax in order to keep it, plus fines for all the rules they had broken. As Ben pulled out his credit card and asked how much, the huge men looked at each other and laughed before they said that money was worthless. But Amanda's anger came as they were shoved into the back of the black SUV, and if there hadn't been a gag in her mouth, she would have told Ben to go fuck himself. Instead, she held five-year-old Violet's hand in hers and tried to make sooth-ing expressions with her eyebrows while her heart pounded in her chest.

The SUV stopped outside the civic center. Amanda hadn't been here since the concert they attended for Ben's birthday and she couldn't parse the difference between the drunken night of flashing lights, and the beat of drums thrumming through her stomach, with this silence and fear. The men in uniform pushed them out onto the sidewalk, pulled their gags, and put headphones on their heads. "Don't take these off," they said. At first, she was happy that she no longer had to listen to Violet humming and hiccupping. She wanted save her baby from any discomfort or hurt. But Amanda tasted bile in her mouth, she was just barely keeping control of her trembling limbs, and a respite from her daughter's terror was a physical relief. The men left them on the sidewalk at the end of a line. A female voice in her ear said, "Proceed to the entry." Amanda searched for the speaker, looked in the windows of the buildings surrounding, but found no one. She tapped Ben on the shoulder and mouthed, "Let's go. Let's run" as she nodded toward the alley.

"It's going to be okay," he said, but she couldn't hear him, she could only see the shapes that his mouth made because the woman in her ear demanded that she move toward the door. Ben headed toward the building and he had Violet's hand, and so Amanda followed, although she found it impossible to stop looking at the alley and her feet, and thinking about how easy it would be to just move in that direction. In the doorway, she grabbed his arm and shook her head. He pushed the earphone off her ear just enough to whisper over the insistent bitch of a woman.

"You're my everything. I will take care of you. I would take a bullet for you and Violet. I know in my gut that this is going to be okay."

She threw up on the floor. It splattered on her shoes. She hadn't thought about the chance of him having to take a bullet. What exactly the payment was, if not money, made her bowels loose.

* • •

The line wound down a hallway. The couples and families were silent and twitchy. Amanda wondered what was coming through Violet's headphones. The girl was wide eyed, but her mouth was finally closed. They shuffled toward a corner, down an even longer hall, and then through a door. The room was semi dark. The door closed behind them. Amanda wanted to press the crash bar to see if it was locked and they were trapped, but instead looked down at Violet and smiled, squeezed her baby's sweaty hand in her own.

There were three families ahead of them. She stretched to see what was happening. Two kiosks with lit panels, like where she used to buy tickets at the movies, sat at the front. The adults were directed to the panels by a middle-aged woman. She was round and brunette. Amanda relaxed a little. The woman was not large, or holding a gun like the men who came to pick them up. She looked like a librarian, or a paralegal. There was a table behind her, but Amanda couldn't see what was on it, the shadows were deep.

The lit panels made her think that they were indeed paying with money. The price must be steep if they had to come in person. It's just money, she told herself. Ben made good money. More than good money. They would be fine. Money solved everything. The people at the front finished on the panels and the woman turned her back and picked up something off the table. Amanda stepped to the right to see. The headphones made her so unaware of her surroundings, that she was startled when she stepped on the foot of a large man in a uniform. She could see the round woman was holding a silver tray, with three small cups. The couple was arguing. The mother of the family put her hands in front of her mouth. The dad swallowed the contents of all of the cups and dropped to the ground. The mom fell too, but a guard grabbed her, and the toddler she was holding, and pulled them from the room. The round woman pressed her fingers to the side of the man's neck, and then another guard carried him out.

Amanda couldn't breathe for the panic rising in her.

Her clothes were soaking wet.

She turned to Ben who was staring straight ahead.

The next couple stepped to the panels; they had no children. They pressed buttons until the woman nodded at them, and they took off their headphones and left. No cups. No one on the floor, or soundless screams. A tiny bit of oxygen made it to Amanda's brain. They could be like that. She felt something hard against her back, pushing her forward.

The couple right in front of them moved to the screens. They, too, had no children. They pressed buttons. The round woman turned to the table, and when she turned back, she had on purple surgical gloves and held a scalpel in her hand. The blade caught the low light. Amanda pulled Violet to her, buried Violet's face in her abdomen as the woman took the man's left ear in a swift slice and laid it on a silver tray. She then pulled out a cleaver and a towel and a grasped the woman by the wrist.

Amanda shook Ben's shoulder but he wouldn't look at her.

She couldn't believe what she saw. She was freezing cold and pinched the tender part of her inner arm so hard she drew blood. This couldn't be happening. He's a web developer and she's an artist for Christ-sakes. They live in the greatest country in the world and paid off their mortgage in six years.

The guard pushed her forward, and pulled Violet from her hands. Amanda forced her eyes to focus on the screen. There was a list of items they must pay for. Too much meat in the freezer. Too much toilet paper. Bags hidden in the closet. Weapons unregistered, concealed. The prices at the bottom. Amanda's stomach rolled. Violet owed her left pinky, but they would also take Ben's or Amanda's in lieu. That's an easy decision, she thought. These bastards aren't touching her daughter. She put her mark next to her own finger.

She owed her right hand. They would also take Ben's hand in exchange for hers. She doesn't even consider this. It's her debt. She put the bags in the closet. She wondered what would happen if they refused to pay. She wondered if that was what the little cups were for. She won't be able to pot, to do the one thing she is called to do, but she will be able to watch Violet grow up. That will be enough. It will have to be. She swallowed hard and thought about the cleaver and the towel. Her legs felt like logs, and she couldn't stop shivering as she put the mark next to her hand in consent. She refused to think about the pain. She kept reading.

Ben owed his right foot.

She thought about him playing in the yard with Violet. About them walking on the beach again someday. Below, it said that they were willing to take her left hand for his foot. She thought about the meat, and the toilet paper, and how he refused to even consider leaving.

She looked at her hands silhouetted against the glow of the panel. She didn't want to make this decision. She couldn't take his foot, but she couldn't make herself completely helpless either. It wouldn't just be the pottery, she thought, she wouldn't be able to cook, hold Violet, or wipe herself. She'd be completely at the mercy of others.

She left it blank and pressed finish.

A bright red star appeared next to the question of Ben's debt. It wouldn't let her finish without answering.

She looked over at him. He was staring at the panel. It's clear to her what they have to do to survive this: sacrifice.

Murmuration, she thinks. That's what it's called.

She wished he would look at her, a smile, a nod, to tell her he understood.

She clicked on her own hand. and before she could change her mind, she clicked finish.

A guard brought a chair and put her down on it. She couldn't see Violet or Ben. The woman came with the gloves, and the cleaver, and the towels. She took Amanda's left pinkie with a thunk. Wrapped a bandage around the bleeding hand. The pain didn't register. Just heat. The woman gripped the bandaged hand and raised the cleaver, she held it over Amanda's left wrist as she made eye contact. Amanda couldn't decide if it was grace or torture that they took the pinkie from the hand that she owed. Surely, they could have made one cut instead of two? Hell, they could remove the pinkie from the hand after.

She was dizzy. She decided that she was just grateful to have one whole hand left as the blade flashed.

It was a crunch this time, not a thunk.

Her arm felt lighter, like she put down a bag of groceries. She took a deep breath. Her left arm began to throb. It's okay, she decided, it's all over now. She can survive this. He promised to take care of her. They will have two hands between them. They will be okay.

The woman put on new gloves, and the snap of the latex drew Amanda's gaze. Then she reached for Amanda's right hand.

Time stopped.

The world stilled and the air shrieked, and a whispered, "no" fell out of her mouth as she realized what he'd done.

When she returned to consciousness, the woman was holding something smelly beneath Amanda's nose, and her head was filled with noise. Amanda realized that the headphones were off. She looked down and her arms were wrapped in gauze, and too short. She dry heaved a little bright yellow bile onto her pants.

"You must have a very good marriage," the woman said.

They were herded back into a van. They weren't gagged this time and they didn't have headphones, but they didn't talk either. Violet stared at Amanda's bandages and refused to touch her mother. Amanda rested her head against the glass of the window.

They were dropped at their house. When they got inside, he walked her to their bedroom and tucked her in. She sweat beneath the blankets, her rage hot and futile. He worked, shopped for groceries, and cooked. She watched TV, opened her mouth when he held a bite of food in front of it. One day as he is changing her bandages, the skin no longer red and angry, but withered, pink and shiny, she said: "I thought you'd take a bullet for me."

"I would."

"Liar."

He said: "I can't take care of you with only one foot. The hand is a lesser loss."

"But both isn't. Didn't you see. If you'd taken my debt, and I'd taken yours. We could have been even." She could see in his face that he knew. He knew and he chose this anyway.

"I told you I'd take care of you," he said. "And I will. You're my everything and I can't lose you."

• • •

In bed, that night, she stared at the ceiling and listened to him breathe, each whistle in, and moan out, built fire in her chest. She could smother him, she thought, her pillow and body weight with the element of surprise might be enough. But she knew, if she couldn't take his foot, she couldn't kill him. But more, she didn't want him dead, she wanted to be even.

She slid from the sheets, and scooped the packs from the hall closet. They should have been unpacked weeks ago, they were risking another inspection, another tax, but Amanda was in no position, and Ben didn't care.

What else could she lose?

She was almost as angry with herself, for not seeing this in him before, for not protecting herself, as she was with him. She knelt beside Violet's bed and kissed her daughter on the forehead until she woke. "I need you to be my hands," she said, before the two slipped silently from the house and into the promise of the night.

And Then the Forest Will Burn Down

*O*ne of the hazards of the job, they say, is bruising around your eyes, from the binoculars. Another, is going crazy, but the trainers spent more time on the binocular techniques - how to balance them without letting your face carry the weight, how to lean on your elbows, or rest them on the glass—than how to preserve one's sanity. Maybe there wasn't anything anyone could do about that. I felt lucky, having some experience with binoculars, being raised by avid birders, but less lucky in that my sanity was in short supply even before arrival.

"You might not care what you look like," he said. "Hell, you might not even know. Not all the cabs have mirrors. But soon your face will hurt. That tender skin under your eyes will ache, and then you're not going to want to use the binoculars or you'll be distracted by pain when you do. And then you'll miss something and then the forest will burn down."

"And then the forest will burn down" was his favorite phrase. Right before "spot and call." The latter was to encourage reporting of every little thing, "no plume too small!" But the former with its visceral image of acres of trees, flattened to blackened ash desolation, established the stakes. I woke to nightmares of woodland animals running through burning tree branches, their eyes wild with terror and their fur smoking; the scent of burning hair stuck in my throat.

"Pay attention," he said. "Watch." Every minute could mean acres, lives and livelihoods. It only takes one spark, one stupid camper, one careless hiker, one stray coal. This wasn't a joke, wasn't easy. Wasn't time to goof off. "Don't get distracted and don't fucking smoke," he said, stubby index finger jabbing the air. I had to hide the snort that escaped when he said that behind a pretend cough. Who did he think I was? How many 40-something women took fire lookout jobs to goof off. To run away from their problems? Yes. Fool around? Not so much.

So, I'd spent the majority of the last month looking out. When I wasn't sleeping, or in the bathroom, I was on the watch deck high above the forest, with my abdomen pressed against the metal rails, my elbows balancing the weight of the binoculars, scanning. Reading my territory like my favorite book. I memorized, learned. I knew those tiny trees, the rock out-croppings, the deadfalls, and the streams better than the topography of my own hand. And when a snake of smoke slithered out, I used the Osborne to map it, and called it in. The voice on the other end of the line, cool and calm. It helped the first time, when my heart beat out of my chest, and I nearly dropped the heavy receiver from my sweaty palm. But eventually, that robotic voice at the other end was just another reminder that I was alone. Yes, my call would set an operation in motion, but I wasn't there. I couldn't see, couldn't pat anyone on the back and say "nice job!" Or "good work back there." No, the best I could hope for was the smoke to just disappear.

Above everything, I watched, and I waited, separate. I knew what I was getting myself into, it was my intention when I applied. When the interviewer asked if I would be okay with long stretches of solitude, when the trainer told me that I wouldn't talk to anyone, not really, for months, I was excited.

I'd wanted the quiet.

• • •

The jeweler on the corner was piping instrumental Christmas songs out onto the sidewalk and the fudge shop smelled of vanilla and burnt sugar. There was a pleasant crisp in the air, just enough to make it feel festive.

"I wish you hadn't worn those heels," he said, dragging her down the sidewalk by the tender inside of her arm.

"I thought you loved these, how they make my legs look."

"In bed. I like them in bed." He looked at his watch. Her heels tapped a rhythm that matched the second hand.

"I don't think they are too sexy for this party. Your boss hardly had any clothes on last year. I saw her nipple twice." Her heel slid into a crack in the uneven pavement and tipped her ankle, and then her body sideways. He gripped harder.

"You can hardly walk. You look drunk. Maybe you're just too clumsy for them?"

"If you would just slow down. What's the rush? The drinks are bottomless. We won't miss the awards, just the soggy mini quiche and the rubber chicken wings."

He didn't answer, just pulled harder. She tried to keep up. By the time they walked through the doors she had sweat at her hairline and on her upper lip.

"Excuse me," she said, breaking away to go to the restroom to check her face. She thought he rolled his eyes as he waved her off, already deep in conversation with a coworker she didn't know. In the bathroom she pressed toilet paper to her face, and ran her wrists under cool water. A young woman emerged from a stall and she suddenly felt ridiculous for trying so hard.

"Hot dress," the girl said, fixing her lipstick that looked almost black in the dim party lighting.

"Thank you," she said smoothing the sequins over her round hips, "Yours, too."

"Damn straight. Gonna get me some," the girl said and left.

She fixed a smudge on her eyeliner. "Stop stalling," she said to the mirror.

She grabbed two drinks on the way back to meet him, pinching her bag under her arm. "Hiding from me," she said when she finally found him in the corner talking to some guy she thought she'd met before. She tried to hand her husband a drink but he shook his head and pointed at the one in his hand. She looked down at the two she was carrying, and around to see if there was anywhere to put one. There wasn't. So, she drank the first drink fast and then nested the cups while the two men talked around her.

"So, Lisa," the other man said finally turning toward her. That wasn't her name but he was clearly speaking to her. "What do you do?"

"She's a teacher," her husband said.

"What do you teach?" said the man.

"English," her husband said.

"That was my worst subject! Nearly got held back in third grade cause I couldn't read. Have you ever had to do that? Hold one of your students back?"

She looked over to see what her husband would say to that. He was all of a sudden very interested in finishing his drink.

"I have had to fail a student before," she said. "But no one gets into graduate school without being able to read."

His eyebrows rose and he looked over at her husband with confusion. "Fuck, Chris," he said. "I didn't know you were the dumb one at your house. No wonder you like hanging around with us knuckleheads." The man turned to her and said, "It was a pleasure to see you again Mrs—"

"Doctor," she said.

He smirked. "Doctor," he said and left.

When she turned to Chris he'd already joined another group and refused to make eye contact with her. She made small talk with his coworkers while he seethed. When it was time to go, she took her shoes off on the sidewalk. Barefoot, downtown

Asheville was better than breaking her ankle trying to run in heels, but still he walked ahead of her.

When she caught up at a stoplight, he said: "I wish you would cut it out with the doctor bullshit. No one cares. They think you're a snob or a bitch."

"It's my name. You used to be proud of me."

"It's just a little much. You're a lot to deal with you know. A lot," he said, and waved his hands in her direction.

• • •

Occasionally, when the wind blew the right way, my cell worked and, messages from my mother would arrive.

I assume you're all right up there.

We miss you. All of us. Even him (I can tell.)

I know you'd tell me if you weren't okay.

Chris dropped off your stuff I put it in the basement.

I turned my phone off and stuck it at the bottom of my duffle with the pack of smokes that I told myself were only for an emergency. I didn't need the distraction of wondering if anyone missed me. If anyone was reaching out. If he was calling? It was better not to know either way.

Silence.

Trees.

Sky.

I watched the horizon obsessively so that I didn't have time to look inside. To pull back my anger and find what lurked behind.

Sometimes birds would land on the rail. I started leaving them some crumbs, but the wind always stole my offerings first. At night in my bunk, I'd press my hands to my cheeks. To my biceps, and belly and thighs just to make sure that I was there. I'd pull my hair gently. I'd explore my teeth with my tongue. I'd listen to the wind whip around my cab, and be grateful. To be here, to be lonely with purpose was better than to be home in bed with him and feeling the same way. My sadness congealed into a stone, a weight that settled into my stomach. It was okay that way though. Easier to carry condensed like that than spread all over my skin.

On the afternoon of the sixty-seventh day, a flag of smoke appeared on the far western ridge of my territory. I went to work. I used the fire finder to map the coordinates, and had just picked up the phone to call it in, when a crackle came over the radio.

I jumped at the sound. It had never done that before. I didn't know it could.

A soft baritone was suddenly in my space. I was instantly aware that I wasn't wearing a bra, and I couldn't remember brushing my teeth.

He introduced himself. Stephen. A lookout neighbor, of course, my cheeks went hot. We compared notes, coordinates. He said he would call it in if I wanted. He said he was pleased to meet me before the radio went quiet in my hand.

I'd been alone for sixty-seven days, but the sudden silence of the radio felt like a blow to my belly. I hadn't thought much about other people for the last two months, about how they sound, or smell. What they feel like, or taste like, hadn't crossed my mind. But now I couldn't stop thinking about how far away the closest body was. How far would I have to go to smell the sweat of another person, to feel the warmth of their skin? If I fell from the tower, if I just didn't wake up tomorrow, how long would it take for someone to notice?

The sun rose and set behind the tops of the trees. I'd never see the bottoms of them. The trunks and roots visible only to those who were willing to spend days trekking, pooping outside, sleeping in the pine needles. The same dry underbrush that would feed a fire would cushion their sleep. For me, the trees really could be anything, at this distance they looked like grass, or aquarium plants, perhaps the edge of a snow globe just waiting to be shaken. I imagined giant hands coming out of the sky and shaking the shit out of me. I wondered where I'd land.

I gave up trying to write.

I climbed up and down the stairs between my living quarters

and the watch deck, noticing the tones the metal made depended on the temperature of the day and my footwear choice.

I practiced holding my breath.

I tried to remember songs I learned in grade school, and shocked myself with how many I could eventually remember all of the words to.

I baked cookies.

I baked bread.

I read the books I brought, and then the books that someone else had left, and then all the manuals for equipment I couldn't even find, and then cereal boxes and shampoo bottles.

I whittled.

I tried to replicate poses from that one yoga class I went to in college.

I made myself spot something that started with each letter of the alphabet: ant, barred owl, cedar, duck, earwig… and got so mad at x that I nearly threw my binoculars over the edge.

Silence.

I spotted three separate smoke wisps and called them in, hoping each time they'd tell me to radio Stephen. But they didn't. I thought of a million excuses to use to call him. But didn't use them. They all sounded stupid when I practiced them out loud, my sweaty fingers wrapped around the radio.

What if he thought I was annoying?

What if he didn't answer?

What if I just imagined the whole thing and there was no one else out there?

• • •

She could tell by the sound of Chris' breathing he was awake. The green number projected on the ceiling said it was after two am and she was just slipping into bed. He didn't roll over to say hi. He wanted her to think he was sleeping. He didn't want to hear about her night. She knew that already. She wasn't allowed to have fun without him. It didn't matter that he hated poets, and worse still, spoken word. He couldn't imagine how she could have fun without him, and she couldn't explain it without hurting his feelings. But still she wanted him to roll over and pull her body tight against his. She wanted to wiggle her ass against his groin and feel the awakening when he put his hand on her hip and discovered she wasn't wearing her pjs, that she wasn't wearing anything.

Instead, she pressed her front to his back. Wrapped her arm around his waist and pulled him tight to her. Kissed the nape of his neck. Then licked.

"What's got you all worked up? Someone read a dirty poem?"

"Maybe." She whispered hooking her bare thigh over his hip and sliding her palm down his stomach. "Take your pants off."

"This isn't for me. Who got you all worked up?"

"It is for you." She licked and bit his shoulder. "I missed you."

"If you missed me, you wouldn't leave me by myself all night." He pulled himself into a tighter and tighter ball.

She rolled onto her back and pulled the blankets up to her neck.

"Sometimes I need to do something that's just for me. Surely you understand that."

"I don't. I don't feel the need to do that. I don't leave you all by yourself."

She sighed, "No, you do your thing with me here, and you make me do it too."

"What's that? What's MY THING?"

"Television. You love television. You watch it constantly and you expect me to watch it with you. To you, it means together time."

"But it doesn't to you?" He rolled over so he was facing her now.

She could feel his anger through the dark. "I don't enjoy TV, so it doesn't feel like enjoyable together time. It feels like something I do for you." She winced as she said it, knowing what it would do.

"I'm sorry I'm not as cultured as you."

"That's not it, I just don't—"

He put his pillow over her face. She wrestled it off.

"I'm not finished."

He took a deep breath. "But you're not the only one who does stuff they don't like to do in order to make their spouse happy."

"What don't you like to do?"

"Plenty."

"Like what?"

"Too many things to name. I don't want to be up all night."

She didn't know what to think. She had a feeling that he was lying, that he was just trying to one up her. That he was still trying to make her feel bad because she'd come home so late. But there was an underlying horror. What if he was doing something for her that he hated as much as she hated watching television? What if he hated it more? She was cold under the blankets. "Why didn't you tell me before?" she whispered.

"I didn't want to make you angry. You're a very angry person and I was afraid of your reaction."

Tears slid out of the corner of her eyes and down her temples. This was not the first time he'd said that.

. . .

The night was close. Damp. Charged. A storm was coming. I was filled with both relief and fear. It had been so dry, the forest was a tinderbox, it was desperate for water. I'd watched everything growing yellow, toasting in the sun for the last two months. I could feel the ground changing, opening itself like a sponge, like a lover, ready for the moisture. But a storm meant lightning, too. One strike in these conditions could be a catastrophe.

My thumb circled the call button. The edge a blade to the soft pad of my flesh. My heart thumped a drumbeat in the silence, as I set the radio down gently and stepped outside, scanning but finding my eyes wandering in the direction I thought he might be. Imagining the far edge of my bubble touching the far edge of his.

The night was black except for occasional lightning illuminating the edges of the clouds in the far distance, not my territory, not his. But the black of the night with no moon, no stars, and the soft feel of the damp air against my skin shrank the vastness, and allowed, for once in so many nights, for me to feel just a little less alone. I knew I should go down to my cabin to get supplies for the night. I would need to stay here and watch for strikes and flares tonight. But I didn't want to leave this feeling. A snap of bright white lit the room, as a strike landed just to the west, followed by a boom of thunder that shook the tower. I was too surprised to move to the fire finder to track it. A sizzle of static came over the radio.

"Did you see that?" he said.

"Yes! Wow," I said.

"Where did it strike?"

"Oh, I don't know."

"I thought you said?… Never mind… Just be on the lookout for more? There will be more," he said.

"I hope so."

I heard air escape through his nose. My cheeks burned at the thought of him laughing.

"I know it gets boring," he said.

"I don't mind boring. I don't mind quiet, or being alone."

"You don't miss people? Conversation? Touching?"

"There's just all this build up. All this tension about what can happen. But it doesn't. Hasn't. Makes me feel like I'm up here for nothing." I couldn't believe I was saying this out loud. Surely he thought I had completely lost it. "Maybe I want to believe that something big can happen and I can be a part of it."

"I think you might miss people more than you know."

The hairs on my arms rose and the palms of my hands tingled as a crack of lightning screamed past, the air sizzled and tasted metallic. It snapped like a whip as it landed between us, and I gripped the handrail watching for a flame as the boom of thunder shook the tower and threatened to knock me off my feet. It was there. Right on top of me. Hope rose in my throat.

"Anything?" The radio fizzled.

I watched. Willing a flicker. Praying for a flame. "No." The breeze was picking up. It blew my hair across my face. The air felt fresher, lighter. I frowned.

Another crack. Further away. Less intense in every way. Disappointment swelled as I counted the seconds before the boom. It was out of my territory now. My radio was silent. I waited until the night was quiet and still before I climbed down the stairs, stripped off my clothes, and fell into bed.

Laying in the dark I thought about the way he said touching. I pressed the palms of my hands to my bare stomach, I thought about how his tongue would have tapped and caressed his teeth and lips as the word formed itself in the warm cave of his mouth. I slid my hands up to my breasts and brushed them gently with the meat of my palm and the tip of my pinky finger. Goosebumps rose on my legs. I thought about whether his eyes would be open or closed and what he would be doing with his hands. I imagined strong hands, with long fingers, stretching across my rib cage and moving up to pinch my nipples, to squeeze my breasts until they ached with a deep fulfilling throb. I imagined a beard, it's soft scratch on my throat, my chest, my belly, and thighs. Big hands gripping my hips, pulling. My palms stroked and fingers slipped over the plains and valleys, the forests of my anatomy. I felt the tension of the last ten weeks, and the years at home before that, build beneath my skin, the bubbles fizzing to the surface, and the heat of my anger roiling it to a boil.

• • •

The oven timer said she had five minutes before she needed to take the cookies out. Too short to leave the kitchen, too long to do nothing. She looked around for a chore she'd been putting off, spied the mountain of unopened mail and sighed. She flipped through the pile.

"Do we need any of these?" she asked Chris who was sitting at the kitchen table reading the newspaper.

"I don't know what THESE are."

"I dunno, bank statements? I think they email those to me. Something from the HOA. Looks like maybe our yearly investment statement."

"If you don't know, they should at least be opened. You threw away our new proof of insurance last month and I had to go through the hassle of requesting a new one. It's not the end of the world to have some extra paper around."

She hated clutter. It itched her skin. She threw away the bank and HOA stuff unopened, but to make him happy opened the investment report. There was way more money in their account than she expected. Like ten times more.

"I think there's a mistake in our investments."

"What do you mean?"

"It's a good one, but, it can't be right. Shit…" she pulled her hands through her hair. "It would be amazing if it was though."

He sighed heavily, "Can you please just tell me what you're talking about. I'm trying to do something here."

"We have way, way more money in our investment account than I thought."

"Oh, that." He turned back to the paper.

"You knew?"

"I did it."

"How?" She couldn't imagine how he could have possibly put more money in their account when she hadn't noticed it coming out of their bank account. She knew that she wasn't the best at keeping track of their finances, but she would have noticed this.

"I moved our nest egg to something higher risk to make a quicker yield. You've been talking about how you want a house before a child, and at the rate we were saving we would never have enough. Not unless you got a better job."

"This is about my job? You risked all our savings because I have a shitty job?"

"Well, you have been talking about quitting, about taking a few years off to write. This makes it so you can. I thought you'd be happy."

"Then why didn't you tell me?"

"Well cause I knew you'd do this."

"This? THIS? You mean ask questions about where my money was and how you were using it? How you were putting our future in danger? THIS?"

"Screaming, yes."

• • •

It didn't help. It didn't calm me. It didn't fill the void in my chest. It didn't soothe the heat from my skin or the roar from my ears. I needed to take more than just my body in my hands. The blankets felt heavy, the cab airless. I climbed the steps to the look out and scanned the horizon. How many nights had I laid in bed at home, with Chris' weight on the mattress, his breath in my nose, waiting? I was tired of waiting. Tired of hoping. I was going to end this standoff. I dumped the duffle on the floor to find my phone buried at the bottom. I pressed the picture of his face and hoped the wind was blowing in the right direction for a signal. It rang and rang. I looked at the time. I hung up and called again.

"Are you okay?" he cleared his throat and answered.

"Yes," I said.

"Jesus Christ, it's three AM!"

There was a murmur. Not Chris. He covered the mouthpiece with something. Muffled conversation seeped through. *The pillow*, I thought.

"It's three AM," he said. "Call back in the morning," and hung up.

I threw the phone into the pitch black of the night. Seemingly ages later I heard it hit something, branches, and then a quiet thud. Dirt. I gripped the rail. I was the one that left. I wasn't allowed to have any expectations.

I needed a drink, but everything was in the cab and I didn't feel like climbing all the way down. I grabbed the cigarettes laying on the floor with the rest of my stuff, and a dirty mug to ash into. Smoking was a big no; I'd have to be careful with my butts.

I lit up, laid down on the grated floor of the watch deck, and watched the smoke swirl into the night. I let my mind follow it. The smoke mingling with the damp breeze and flying off to new adventures. Maybe that was what I needed. Something to set my heart racing—surfing, maybe, rock-climbing. Intentional adrenaline, instead of this purposeless boredom I'd created. I needed to create my own heat to combat the creeping chill of my failing marriage.

I lit another cigarette. And another. Heart racing, hands shaking, I watched the flame born at the end of my lighter catch and die, catch and die. I'd been so cold for so long. Numb. How exciting it had felt, when I'd let the anger take me.

Yes, I thought. *Yes.*

And then I rolled over, and dropped the lit cigarette through the floor grate, watched its descent through the night to land on the pine needles below, and waited, the tender flesh of my face pressed hard to the metal, focused despite the pain, for something to happen.

I watched. Deep breaths filling my lungs, filling my belly. In and out.

And there it was, a tiny ember, a miniature orange sun glowing beneath me. It gathered energy from the surrounding dry needles and twigs. Growing from a small ember to a flame. I scrambled down the tower stairs, my footsteps pounding through the night, afraid and excited about what my fire might be when I got to it. Praying that it didn't put itself out. Praying it had more strength than I did.

It was still small when I knelt beside it. Even after I blew on it. Even after I threw handfuls of fuel on it. But it wasn't when I called it in, when I relayed the coordinates and heard the catch in the voice on the other end.

Here in the Dark

Cora's Story

*I*t had been three months since she'd had a drink. Twelve weeks since she'd pulled smoke into her lungs. Ninety days without a needle, or a pill, or a bump. But it wasn't her hunger for drugs or alcohol that had Cora sweating on the sidewalk in front of Mountain Rehab, but her desperate need to sit on Lee's face.

The man was magic; goosebumps rose all over her body thinking of his fingers, and his tongue. A vision of his shirtless torso, the hair on his chest, his jeans low on his hips revealing an arrow of muscle pointing down. Cora had to close her eyes and take a deep breath. He was so, so good, but they were even better together. Lightning. Forest fires. An earthquake flattening a city block. Pompeii. The memory of the heat of his mouth on hers was the only thing that was any distraction from the pain of withdrawal. The thought of his arms holding her in the dark the only thing that kept her from disintegrating into a thousand pieces as the therapists and counselors attempted to pick her apart. The dream of a future together the only thing that made any of this worth it. She'd get clean. They get married. She'd get her son back and then her very own happily ever after. After everything she'd survived, everything she'd caused, she wasn't sure that she would ever get this, that the universe would ever allow this, yet, there was Lee, and he was her everything. So, the fact that she'd been standing here, finally free and waiting for him for over an hour, was concerning.

It was a knife twisting in her gut that there was no one else to call, no one else who would be excited that she was out of rehab. She'd lived the kind of life where people didn't miss her, where they were relieved when she left the room. It never stopped hurting. It also wasn't exactly true. She could have called her brother. He and her son would be happy that she was out. Too happy though, that's why she couldn't see them yet. They would get their hopes up that she was going to be a sister and a mom, they would think that they could count on her, trust her, and then she would fuck everything up doing something stupid like getting drunk on shoplifted wine in the bathroom at Ingles and throwing up all over the display of local apples. She couldn't handle being a disappointment yet again. She needed to get her shit together before she came back to them.

So, she'd only told Lee. There were too many other people she needed to avoid. And Lee had said he wouldn't miss it for the world. He said he'd camp out the night before like they had before that Allman Brothers concert. Twenty-four hours on that side walk, taking turns holding each other up as they slept, eventually giving up and laying on the cement after they'd had enough beers to forget about the poking pebbles and the dirty looks. The concert had been worth it though, the red stage lights reflecting off Lee's face. His hands in her pockets. Cora had held her arms above her head in rapture for so long that she couldn't move them the next day and Lee had had to hold her sandwich in front of her face so she could take bites.

But she was alone. She must have told him the wrong date, they all blended together inside. That was it, she thought, chewing her cuticle. She wandered down the block to a payphone and called the taxi. When she climbed in the backseat and gave the driver the address his shoulders dropped. He took his hands off the wheel and met her eyes in the rearview mirror.

"I'm good for it," she said.

"That's a long way."

"I promise," she said.

"Won't have no one to pick up out there. I'll be empty all the way back."

"I'll give you a big tip."

He sighed, and put the car in drive as he shook his head. Cora tapped her nails against the window. It had only been three months, not that long, and yet so much had changed. Asheville had gotten bigger. Buildings were taller. Lights brighter. Cars louder and faster. And the city itself had spread; new structures where before there'd just been dirt. She was always in the way in this new busy city, bumping into something or someone she shouldn't. Women held their purses tight to their bodies as they gave her a wide berth. Men leered, or looked down their noses. She ached for the quiet of Lee's place, the enveloping dark of his porch at night, the calming trill of cicadas and peepers, and knowing exactly where she should be: sitting in Lee's lap, his hand on her ass, and her head on his chest.

Gravel crunched beneath the cab's tires as it pulled in beside Lee's F-150. Cora couldn't help the fizzle of excitement that ran through her body. Her man was just on the other side of that door, and she was going to see him, touch him, hold him, and for the first time she was sober, and not hungover or going through withdrawals. She threw a handful of wrinkled bills at the driver, grabbed her duffel and dashed out of the door. At the top of the stairs the cabbie honked, and Cora turned to see him shaking his head. So her tip hadn't been as generous as she'd let on, but what did he think? He knew where he picked her up. He shouted out the window and flipped her off. She shrugged; nothing was ruining her mood.

She knocked, and listened, nothing. Wiped her palms on her jeans. Knocked harder. Footsteps approached and her heart nearly came out of her mouth. Lee opened the door wide, stood shirtless and barefoot. His jeans hanging on his hips, hair wet, toothbrush in his mouth.

"Goddamn," she said, dropping her bag and leaping into his arms, wrapping her long legs around his waist. Lee didn't bother pushing the door shut, he just carried her into the bedroom.

Cora landed flat on her back on Lee's comforter. It smelled like him. It smelled like home. His mouth was on hers. His stubble rough against her cheek, her chin. His tongue in her mouth. His lips between her teeth. She wanted her mouth, her throat, her whole body filled with him. Her hands reaching out like tentacles, his chest, his shoulders, his jaw, and hair. Her fingertips hungry for the textures of him. Thighs squeezing, legs tangled. She pulled everything in, she was a black hole of want, of need, for Lee.

His mouth went to her jaw. Her collarbone. A moan escaped. This was more than missing him, this was a hunger. His lips and teeth and tongue explored her ribs and then her belly. His hands working ahead of his mouth to free her of clothes, to bare the trail.

He pushed her left knee to the side and dove in.

He hummed.

She groaned.

He did this thing with his mouth where he latched on and no matter how she rolled and bucked he didn't get go. Her body felt carbonated, and he just shook her and shook her and shook her, until she exploded.

She knew what people said about her, that she lived her life on her back, but that was bullshit. That was working. She didn't lay there, that's what their wives did. And she didn't get off. There was nothing sexy about her work. Nothing fun. If she had to, if it was important to some john to pretend that he was really good at this, she faked it, but it was all a part of the ruse. Everyone sold a part of themselves to put food in front of their children and a roof over their heads, with Cora it was just more obvious which part that was.

"God, you taste good," he said.

She tangled her fingers in his hair.

So, this was rare, this pleasure, this vulnerability. It had taken Lee a long time to earn it, but she was so glad that he did. She'd never been able to see a future before Lee. She'd never imagined being able to get clean. To have someone support her unconditionally. She hadn't felt that since before her parents died. Her fingers tightened in his hair. She moaned and then her body melted into a puddle.

He dropped his pants and slid inside her. She wrapped her arms around his neck and her thighs around his waist and she squeezed. She wanted to feel his heartbeat against her breasts. To watch his pupils expand as his body went rigid and then collapsed on top of her hers.

He wiggled his hips.

"I'm not letting you go," she said.

"Okay," he said, letting the full weight of his body press her into the mattress.

"Point made!" she squeaked, and then he rolled to the side. But she couldn't stand the distance between their bodies, so she followed and hooked her thigh over his hip, her hands on his chest. "I missed your smell," she said, breathing deeply, pulling his breath and his scent inside her. "And your taste," she said, licking his lips. "And how warm you are," she said, pulling his torso against hers. "I feel like I've been freezing for three months."

"We both know you mean my cock."

She laughed so hard she snorted. She looked into his eyes. "Why weren't you there?"

"I musta got the wrong time."

"I waited, I thought you didn't care."

"I just messed up the time, honest. I even cancelled plans. I just thought it was later. I swear. I swear on Phil Niekro's arm."

"Okay," Cora said. "Ok." She believed him. There weren't many things Lee loved more than his Braves.

She rolled over so he could spoon her, pulled his arms around her, pressed her ass into his groin. This was what she missed most. This safety. "I don't remember those," she said, pointing at a pile of beer cans stacked neatly on his dresser. "You've been doing a lot of drinking in bed?"

"Oh no. They're from my truck. I had to clean it." He said, into the bend of her neck.

"But you brought the empties in here?" She wondered if maybe he'd gone a little bit crazy while she was away. She knew he'd be lonely. She didn't think he'd be that lonely.

"They're not just empties, they're special. See that one," he said, pointing to what appeared to be just a regular Budweiser can. "That's the beer I was drinking when you finally noticed me at that party."

"You mean that was the kind of beer?"

"No, that was the can. I kept it. Threw it in my truck so I wouldn't forget. The PBR is from our first date, kiss and I guess fuck, too! That Budweiser," he said, pointing to another regular looking can, "was one I got when I met Cash. When we went to the baseball game. That one beside it was when we went fishing and you fell in and your white top got wet, and goddamn if I didn't fall in love with you right there."

Cora started crying. He was just too much. She spent so much of her life trying to forget. Trying to erase memories with beer and drugs, and here this doofus was doing just about everything he could to remember. To remember her. She kept his face in her palms, "I'm in love with you," she said and for the first time, meant it.

. . .

Cora couldn't be sure if it was the vibration of the girl's screams, or if it was the heat of the girl's anger that woke her. But one minute Cora was sleeping, naked, wrapped in Lee's arms, and the next she was wide awake and tiny brunette was standing at the foot of the bed, hollering and yanking the blankets and sheets from Cora's body.

"You motherfucking worm! You piece of shit!"

It took Cora a moment to realize that the almost woman was screaming at Lee and not at her.

"Michelle," Lee stuttered. "How'd you get in here?"

"The front door was wide-fucking-open, you're lucky I'm not a goddamn bear. I hope your fucking house is full of snakes and possum."

"Shit," Lee said, sitting up and rubbing his face.

"This," Michelle said, pointing at Cora, her arm outstretched like an arrow. "This is why you couldn't come to Mama and Daddy's? Mama made mac and cheese! I made peach cobbler!"

This was a tantrum if Cora had ever seen one. The girl did everything but stomp her foot and beat her fists on the floor. Cora slowly moved into a sitting position and picked up her t-shirt from the floor, sliding it over her arms and her head. There was a baseball bat leaning against the wall behind the bedroom door, not two feet from Michelle's fingers. Cora knew what she would do if she was Michelle, and she knew that she should not be naked when that happened.

"Baby," Lee said.

"What?" both women said. And Cora felt fire flash through her body. Why was this child answering to that?

"Shit," Lee said. "I can explain."

Both women crossed their arms across their chests but for Cora it was so that she didn't grab his hair with her fists and beat his skull off the headboard.

He turned to Cora. Held his arms in front of his body like he knew she was going to hit him. "I didn't mean to. I mean it wasn't planned. You left and I was lonely-"

"I didn't leave, I got ordered to rehab by a judge." She poked her index finger into his shoulder until he winced.

"Okay, okay. But I was lonely and so I just went out to be with people. Not even specifically women. I just went out with the guys. I was just shooting pool at the Wolf and then Michelle was there and we started talking."

"She's not screaming at you in your bedroom cause you chatted her up over a pool table."

Lee looked like he might throw up.

"She's like what 12? Why were you messing around with this child?"

"I'm seventeen," Michelle said and Cora rolled her eyes.

"Please, I have jeans older than you."

"Old enough to give him the baby that you can't."

Cora snorted. "Who said I can't have babies? I got one already."

"He did. He said you wouldn't be able to stay clean long enough and that if you all made a baby it would end up fucked up like your kid."

Cora threw her body at Michelle and held the girl against the wall by her neck.

"Don't," screamed Lee. "She's pregnant," he jumped out of bed and put his body between the women.

"What?" Cora braced herself against the wall. "You knocked up this baby. What the fuck is wrong with you?"

"Maybe it's what's wrong with you," Michelle said from behind Lee.

"You better do something about her mouth before I break all them pretty teeth," Cora said to Lee.

Lee dragged Michelle out of the bedroom and Cora could hear them whispering before the front door slammed. Cora put her pants on. She grabbed the baseball bat.

"I can explain," he said, standing naked in the bedroom doorway. "I—"

She swung the bat and broke the mirror over the dresser. She thought that the glass raining down would make her feel better, but it wasn't enough. She swung back again to take a crack at the window but Lee caught the end of the bat. "Come on now," he said. She held on, searching his face for something other than exhaustion. After a minute she dropped her end.

"Is she really pregnant?"

He nodded.

"Is it yours?"

He nodded again; his shoulders slumped.

Cora felt a sharp pinch in the bridge of her nose and looked up so she wouldn't cry. "All that stuff last night was bullshit? You're a good fuck, you know? I've been alone for three months. I would have put out without the love stuff."

"I do love you. Michelle was a mistake."

"But you want the baby?"

He sighed, and nodded.

Cora sat on the end of the bed. Figured that this would be her undoing, she'd finally found a guy who wanted a family, and now it was being used against her. She counted to four as she breathed in, and then to four again as she breathed out. He put his hand on her shoulder and she just about near jumped out of her skin. He couldn't touch her. She didn't want to hear his voice. She needed to get out of there before she broke something else. She collected her things while he stood there stupidly and she tried not to pay attention to how good his body looked or how cute his bedhead was. He followed her to the door. On the porch she turned and asked, "did you really talk shit about my kid?"

He looked down at the floorboards. He didn't see it coming when she punched him in the face.

• • •

Her parents died when Cora was in high school, and her brother Chuck gave up everything to take care of her. A football scholarship, probably girlfriends, definitely freedom. No twenty-year-old man is excited to have his teenaged sister in his custody, but especially a little shit like Cora. She'd cut more class than she attended. She'd skipped out in the middle of the night so often that he'd nailed her window shut and took to sleeping in a recliner outside her door. She'd sold all of their mom's jewelry for drug money and was halfway through their dad's tools when a padlock appeared on the shed door. He'd yelled, she'd screamed, and more than one tub of margarine had exploded against the kitchen wall. She'd made his life miserable, because she was, because she could. She told herself that Chuck didn't need any more of her bullshit, that he'd already put up with a lifetime's worth of heartbreak because of her, and that's why she didn't go knock on his door. Instead, she found a trick and after asked him for a ride up the mountain to an old friend's. An old friend who had put Cora through an equal amount of shit, they were even, so Cora felt like she could ask for a favor.

Dottie's trailer was disgusting, but Cora had nowhere else to go, and Dottie always had drugs. Cora had forgotten that Dottie was knocked up though, and apparently that meant she only had the natural stuff now. Cora held the smoke from the joint deep in her lungs before she blew it out into the haze that was already collecting.

"I'd have killed him," Dottie said. She was wearing a dress that had been short before she tried to smuggle a basketball beneath it. The way she was sitting, with her leg over the arm of the sofa, Cora could see her underwear.

"I might."

"Right on," said Dottie nodding aggressively.

"I don't want him to die, though, you know? I just want to hurt him." She passed the joint back and leaned back into the lawn chair that Dottie saved for guests.

"Burn down his house?"

"Shit, you're full of ideas. That seems cowardly, don't it? And I want to live in that house. I just want him to see me. To know my pain. To regret hurting me. And you know…"

"Leave her and come crawling back."

"Yeah."

Cora was drifting off when she heard Dottie say, "poison."

* * *

Cora woke, her body so stiff it felt like an old bicycle, or a frozen chicken wing, or that fucking protractor she could never get to work in tenth grade geometry, from sleeping in Dottie's goddamn lawn chair. She wasn't on the street, but she wasn't at Lee's. She needed to fix that, to make him see the error of his ways.

Dottie's man offered Cora a ride down the mountain and she took it. She had him drop her off at the post office for privacy but what she really wanted was to see her baby, so she crossed the street and hung out at the elementary school fence. She'd all sorts of bad memories about this place. That bitch Ms Smith never cut her any slack. She wondered if Cash was a good student. He was smart. She could tell that even when he was a baby, he would recognize things, put tough puzzles together, and remember words easily. But neither Cora nor Chuck had much motivation for school. She'd really fucked that up. She hadn't left Cash with much, red hair and too many freckles, a bad attitude towards anyone telling him what to do. But she left him with Chuck, who could fix just about anything, and she hoped that was enough.

The bell rang and kids flooded the schoolyard. She could see him, a full head taller than the other kids, leaning against some sort of climbing structure, rubbing the toe of his shoe in the dirt. She wanted to run over and say hi, to reach her fingers through the chain link and touch him. She didn't much care about what the court said. She had already broken a dozen of their rules, but she didn't want to hurt Cash. Didn't want to raise his hopes that she was home. So, she watched from a distance until the bell rang and he loped back inside. She remembered the scent of his skin. How he used to scream bloody murder when he was hungry, and he was always hungry. She remembered the weight of him in her arms and the way that he used to rub his nose on her collarbone when he was sleepy, and tangle his fingers in her hair. She'd never experienced that kind of love before. He was completely vulnerable and completely dependent on her, but his expectations were so low. Food. The warmth of her body. The sound of her voice. The parameters of his love didn't change, it didn't depend on who was in charge at work, or a new pretty face at the bar, or whether she could score. She just had to show up. And she'd fucked up something as easy as that.

Lee didn't love that girl, and they could cross the problem of that baby bridge when they got to it. She loved Lee. He had made a mistake and everybody deserved a second chance. At least that was what her lawyer had told the judge anyway. She'd go over there and fix it. She took the shortcut through the park that dumped her into Lee's backyard. He'd be at work. She'd clean up, make him some dinner, and show him what a good little housewife she could be.

. . .

She heard it through the open window before she could see anything. The unmistakable slap of sweaty bodies coming together. Her stomach and her fists tightened into knots. She climbed the stairs to the deck and confirmed what she'd feared. Michelle on top of her man. And her man participating with great enthusiasm.

The back door was locked. He'd learned his lesson. She thought about diving through the window screen, and then she remembered the tool shed.

She yanked open at the shed door and dust fell into her face, irritating her eyes and sticking to the sweat on her brow. The lighting was poor and she didn't know where he kept anything. She tripped over something that dumped and a chemical smell filled the space making it even harder to breathe. She felt her way around until she found his workbench. First, she found a crowbar, and she thought she could use it to pry open the door. Then she found an awl, and thought it might be useful on the lock. She smiled and ran back to the house.

Then she saw it, Lee's precious truck, gleaming red like a cherry in the sun.

The plastic and glass of the right tail light made a very satisfying smash when she hit it with the crowbar. The left was even better. The flappy hiss of the left side tires when she stabbed them with the awl made her laugh out loud. The awl got stuck in the front right tire, and she hated to abandon it, but by then Lee was screaming at her from the window and she knew she needed to hurry. She got the driver's window, and then used the bumper as a step to climb up on the hood. She raised the crowbar above her head like she was about to kill a snake. He was suddenly next to the truck, shirtless, like always.

"Goddamn it, Cora. What the hell are you doing?"

Cora looked to the front door where she saw Michelle standing, wrapped in the sheet. She swung the crowbar. The windshield turned white beneath the metal, and a spider web of cracks spread across the glass.

"Stop! Stop!" He hollered as she raised the bar above her head again and swung, only this time, instead of a satisfying smash, there was a thud.

"Fucking Hell! Jesus Christ, you hit me." Lee said, his upper body spread part way across the windshield, a raw red welt raising on his shoulder and upper back. She paused, grimacing. Before Cora knew what was happening, someone had her by the ankle, and yanked her off the hood of the truck and onto the ground. The impact emptied her chest of air, and she couldn't scream when she found Michelle, barely clad in the bed sheet, on top of her hitting her in the face. But Cora had six inches, fifty pounds, ten years, and a lifetime of bar fights on the girl. Cora bucked her off and was on top of her in a moment, pressing the girl to the pavement with the crowbar over her throat.

And that's how the police found her when they arrived.

"Really?" she said to Lee as they cuffed her and put her in the car.

"Neighbor," he said, holding his shoulder and wincing. "Sorry."

The heat of Cora's anger steamed the windows of the cruiser as they drove her to the station.

. . .

She sat across the table from a handsome middle-aged man in

a suit. If he'd tried to pick her up at the bar she would have let him. But here, in this tiny room with its two-way glass and shitty coffee, Cora wasn't feeling like playing nice.

He introduced himself as a detective but she didn't remember his name and wasn't sure if it mattered. She was also pretty sure that a detective wasn't necessary for a simple assault charge. Her teeth rubbed hard against each other. She was so fucking stupid. Assault, and with a weapon she bet, that goddamn crowbar. At least she was sober, and not carrying. She bit her nails for something to do, and to stop the pain in her jaw from grinding her teeth.

"Cora, I can see this isn't your first time here," he said tapping the outside of a thick manilla folder. "So, I won't bore you. What these charges could do, if they make it to a judge, is put you in jail for a really long time. You have a son, right? Maybe with good behavior you'd be out in time to see his kids grow up. Maybe. That is if he even remembers you after all that time. And don't think we're going to have any trouble proving you did what you did, weren't too sneaky about it, right out there in the driveway. I'm kind of impressed, actually, that's ballsy. You're my kind of girl."

It was all Cora could do not to roll her eyes.

"So, I have a proposition for you. And I know you get all sorts of those, so let me be clear, it's very specific. There's a problem in this county that you can help me solve. And if you help me. I'll help you." She listened to him describe his plan, incredulous, but his mouth just kept moving, his pointer finger jabbing the table top, his eyes large and focused on her.

"You're giving me a deal?" She asked. She didn't believe it. She didn't know anything deal worthy.

"If that's what you want to call it, sure. The important part is that you're going to provide me with a very specific type of information, and if you do, in return, I'm not going to put this file on Judge James' desk."

Cora rubbed her face with her hands. Bounced her legs under the table. Tried not to get her hopes up.

"Deputy Cutsforth is going to come in and wire you up later. I'm sorry we don't have a female officer, but as you can imagine with this case, it's very delicate, I can't risk a leak."

"I hate the sound of my voice," she said. She didn't want him to get his hopes up either. She was a fuck up. The chances of this going right were nearly nil.

"You won't have to listen to it."

"I won't be able to sound natural if it's there. He'll be able to tell."

"Honey, girls in your profession are the best actors there are. Convincing those schmucks that you're having a good time? Or that you've never done this before? Or that you're not repulsed by their poor hygiene? If you can do that, you can do this."

Cora chewed on her nail. He was right. She could talk to anyone. She could be incredibly convincing. Could she really make this mess go away just doing this one thing? "What's the catch," she said, eyes narrow, watching his face. "This seems too easy."

"I didn't say easy. But it is pretty simple, and I believe you can do it. Even if the only reason is that you want to see that boy of yours again."

She couldn't let Cash down again. It wasn't the look of disappointment that shadowed his face when she fucked up. She deserved that one. It was the look of hope he beamed every time she saw him that killed her. She didn't merit his trust, she wanted to, but she didn't. And the fact that he was going to give it to her every time just cut her in half. She lived in fear of the time when she showed up and he wasn't excited.

"Who's the guy?"

"Robert William Jackson III," he said, tapping the end of his pen on the table.

"Thought you said I knew him?"

"You probably know him as just Jackson."

"Fuck," she said. This wasn't going to be easy or simple.

• • •

She told them that to see Jackson she needed a shower, and her clothes that were at Lee's. They sent a car for her stuff and let her shower in the jail, but wouldn't let her leave, so Cora was sure that Jackson would be able to tell that she'd washed her hair with jail soap, and hopefully he wouldn't notice the prickles on her underarms or her legs cause they wouldn't give her a razor. Maybe it had been long enough that he wouldn't remember how cute she once was. She was counting on his nostalgia, so maybe she should play up the recovering junkie part to explain her looks. She had put on a little weight in rehab and it had gone to all the right places, thank God.

Cutsforth came in to help set up her mic. He had dead blue eyes and was silent the whole time as he taped the wires to her sweaty skin and her stomach rolled in his proximity. At the very end, he leaned close to her ear, and whispered so quiet she couldn't be sure if he said: "He could kill you," or "He should kill you."

• • •

An unmarked car dropped her around the corner from Jackson's bar, the Howling Wolf. Cora couldn't stop thinking about the electronics she was carrying. She wondered if whoever was listening was close enough to hear her, if she should whisper a test to them to see if she could see a response. They didn't give her any sort of instructions about what to do if she was in trouble. She imagined if Jackson caught her, there wasn't much they could do. The knowledge made her esophagus tight.

"Long time no see," Billy Ray the doorman said. He was Jackson's first line of defense and Cora needed him to be on her side.

"Hey Billy, you're looking good." He blushed. "You got another one of those?" She pointed at his cigarette.

"Only for you," he said.

She let him light it for her, and bent over just enough so that he could down see down her top a little, but not enough to see what was taped to her stomach. The detective had been annoyed that they had to place the mic so far from her mouth. He thought she was playing some sort of game, but she knew she'd need to use her tits if she was going to be able to get this done. She'd also picked a really short skirt, knowing if Jackson decided he wanted under it, it was more likely that he would just push it up than get her to strip naked. She regularly made these kinds of wardrobe decisions, what type of shoe could be used as a weapon against a john? Which type of dress was the easiest to get back on in the dark, or in tight location, but the consequences had never been so dire.

"How you been?" she said, leaning against the metal siding of the building.

"Can't complain," he said. "Looking forward to taking my dogs hunting next month. Training a new one and he's a beast."

"That's cool," she said blowing smoke.

"You ever seen a coon get treed? It's a beautiful thing."

"Can't say I've ever had the pleasure."

"You should come!" He said in a rush, his eyes bright in the glow of the sign above the door.

"I'd like that," she said, crossing her arms under her breasts and pushing them up. "Say is Jackson in there? I got a message he's looking for me."

Billy frowned. "He is, but I didn't know he was looking for you. Not that he wouldn't want to see you." He blushed again.

"Well you can imagine he might not be my first choice of dinner date."

Billy Ray nearly glowed with embarrassment. He'd been Jackson's man for a long time. Since before Jackson had seduced a teenage Cora. Before she thought she was in love with him. Before Jackson got her hooked on the hard stuff and then pimped her out. Before he tossed her into the street because her habit had become a liability. Billy Ray wasn't terribly bright, but he knew that Cora wouldn't be here willingly.

"But if you wants to see you…"

"Exactly," she said. "I come running."

"Well good luck with that," he said, with a wincing smile, opening the door and letting her pass through.

The bar was dark, and loud, and sticky, just like she remembered it. She supposed it was nice that some things didn't change. Jackson was in the back corner booth sitting across from his right man hand man Roy. Roy was a snake in human form. Sneaky, slithery, and he could make your skin crawl just thinking about where you might find him. Despite the terrible shit that Jackson had put her through, Roy made her glad that Jackson had claimed her. Too many girls fell asleep during dates with him, and woke in the backseats of their own cars needing to go to the emergency room to get fractured jaws set, or perineal sutures. But Jackson was a hippo, deceptively dangerous, and Cora had been crushed by his blunt jaws before. She needed to play this real careful. She needed to see Cash again.

She put some extra swing in her hips as she strode across the bar and climbed onto his lap. She straddled him, knowing with her ass in his hands and her boobs in his face he'd be a lot more pleasant to talk to.

"Miss me," she said, her hands on his cheeks.

"Hell, yes," he said leaning back to get a good look at her. He was trying to figure out how fucked up she was, she knew.

"You didn't visit me," she pouted.

"What happened to Lee?" he said grinning.

Cora wondered how much of Michelle ending up in Lee's path had to do with Jackson. She cut eyes at him, "He's pedophile."

"Children like children," Jackson said. "You need a man."

"Why do you think I'm here?"

"Well," he said rubbing his chin. "I'd say you need drugs or money. Fortunately…"

She kissed him hard. Sucked his lower lip into her mouth like he liked. "Let's go somewhere quieter," she said.

Jackson nodded, and Cora wasn't going to question her good luck, so she took his hand and pulled him out of the booth.

"You ain't even going to like frisk her or nothing?" Roy asked. "Damn man, pussy can't be that good. She could be packing."

Cora was sure the technicians could hear her heart pounding through the mic. "Nice to see you again, Roy," she said, dusting her words with sugar.

Jackson smiled sideways at Cora, "you carrying, baby?"

"Do I need more than these?" she asked nodding down at her breasts.

"No, ma'am," Jackson said. "See," he looked at Roy. "You satisfied?"

"Not hardly," said Roy, taking a swig out of his bottle. "It's your ass."

A drip of sweat rolled down the back of her neck. Seconds passed like hours as she waited for Jackson to end this. It had to be his idea. She couldn't push, it would be suspicious. Jackson looked at her, and then at Roy, and then back to her. She took his hand, and put it under her skirt, and pressed it against the heat of her.

"No panties," he said, eyebrows up in the middle of his forehead.

"I ain't got nothing to hide."

Flames blazed in his eyes, "Let's go," he said and pulled her into the parking lot and into his truck.

"Oh this is nice," she said running her fingers over the leather. "Business must be good."

"A lot has happened since you've been gone."

"I was only in rehab three months."

"That's not what I meant," he said, turning the engine over.

"We don't got to go nowhere," she said. "This is fine in here. Smells better than my place anyway. That new car thing they all talk about, I guess."

"Nah, it's been a long time. I'm going to take you to my place where no one will bother us."

"All the way out to your place? I hope you got some snacks?" She hoped whoever was listening got that. This had just gotten a lot more complicated.

"I'll take care of you, baby. Don't I always. How's our boy?" Cora's teeth snapped closed. She wasn't going to dignify that with a response. She looked sideways at Jackson. "He need something? Probably shoes? Growing like a weed! Probably eating Chuck out of house and home. You living with them? Or did Chuck kick you out too? Is that why you came back? Chuck kicked you out? Lee shacked up with that wee thing and so you came running back to Daddy?"

"They're not shacked up."

"That's not what I heard."

Cora wondered if Jackson cared enough about her to have stuck his nose in the Lee and Michelle situation. She didn't think so. They had a lot of history but he had kicked her out. If anything, Lee did Jackson a favor getting Cora off the street and out of his hair. "Why do you care about Lee? He's small potatoes. That's what you always told me. You run with the big boys. And this ride, shit. I believe you."

He nodded and smiled.

"Come on. You're honestly not going to tell me? You driving this around town. It isn't a secret."

"Nope, nope it ain't sweetheart." He pulled into his driveway and pulled her onto his lap. His hands were everywhere and she prayed that he was too excited about their reunion to pay much attention to the lumps and bumps under her clothes. She had to admit he was a fun time. He looked soft but he wasn't. Former farm boy muscle covered in a few to many beers, but his body felt good, solid. He threw her over his shoulder, bare ass to the sky, as he carried her into the house. He set her on the kitchen counter, and started unbuckling his belt buckle.

"Hey now," she said. "You bring me all the way out here, and now you're in a hurry? Where's my tour? I should at least get a beverage."

He pulled two beers out of the fridge, popped them open and handed one to her. "Cheers," he said, clicking the bottle necks together. "To… what? Reunions? Second chances? Old friends?"

"That's more like it," she said looking around. "You've renovated since I was here last."

"Had to."

"Why?"

"Wouldn't you like to know." He winked at her and ran his hand up her thigh.

Cora was sweating. "There's a lot more of them critters, too." She nodded to the wall covered in taxidermy.

"I'm getting pretty good, ain't I? You know I got these magical fingers." He wiggled his fingers at her. She knew exactly what he could do with them and stuffing dead animals was not the worst thing. She thought about how much money he'd spent on those stupid ugly animals. And how poor women weren't allowed to have hobbies. Sure, someone would say that baking, or sewing, or quilting, or canning were a hobby, but they weren't, they were just ways to exist. Ways to stretch a dollar, or something to barter. No poor woman gardened for pleasure. Maybe rich women kept bees for fun. Or foraged mushrooms for the hell of it. But no poor woman had the resources—time or money—to hunt a prize and then pay to hang it on her wall. *Fucking assholes* she thought, about men who had the ego to be so fucking wasteful and stupid. "That's an awful big TV over there. You got to tell me what game it is you're playing."

"You got a lot of questions." His eyes were narrow, still sparkling, still playful, but she knew he was smart and mean and she was right on the edge.

"Maybe," she said biting her lip. "Maybe a girl is trying to figure out if she's with the wrong man?"

He smirked, rubbed his palms together. "Well, I got an offer for you. You asked me a question, I'll answer it, but in return you take off a piece of that there outfit."

Cora did the math. She had two questions, her bra and her skirt. Anymore and she needed to take off her top, and she couldn't do that. Two questions to get enough info that the cops would clear her slate. It seemed near impossible but she was here, so she was going to have to fuck him and let them listen, anyway. She could do her best, first. "I remember," she said, "way back in the day. Back when we first started to hang out, you said that the fastest way to fuck a guy was to make him think that he was in charge."

"Did I? I used to say wise things, I guess."

"So I'm just saying, I know what you're doing. But, you know, getting fucked is what I came here to do…" She made her eyes real big and slid off the counter.

"Shew, baby," Jackson said and followed her into the living room.

She pushed him down on the couch, and stood with her legs apart, and her hands on her hips. "Where's all the money from?"

"Business," he said stretching his arms out along the top of the couch cushions. "I'm an excellent negotiator. I understand supply and demand."

"Of what?"

"That's another question. You got to take something off first."

She reached behind her and unclasped her bra and pulled it out of the neck of her shirt. "Ooh, that's cheating," he said. "I like it."

She threw the bra him.

"Do you still want me to answer that? Or was that a mistake, you don't look like you have too many questions left."

"What are you selling?" That would be enough for the cops, surely. If he named any of the many illegal things that he peddled in, that would be enough, she thought.

"Whatever you want. You think I'm being evasive. I'm not.

Whatever you want. I can get it for you. So, let's just go with everything. Now you, show me something good."

She started to unbutton her skirt. Fucking shit, she thought, she screwed that up. She slid the material down her legs and then twirled so he could admire and she could think. "I heard," she said, index finger in her mouth, her other hand sliding up her inner thigh, "there was a cop involved? That missing cop? You know where he is?" She watched his face. His eyes narrowed and his lips turned down. His cheeks were a purple color and his hands made fists on his knees. "Is the bathroom still this way?" she said pointing at the other end of the house and dashing away.

"Oh! Woman! You're killing me," he said as she locked the door. She ripped the wire off and dropped it in the toilet, and crammed the battery pack behind a pile of junk under the sink. She was still sitting on the seat, trying to catch her breath and figure out her next step when the door crashed open. Jackson stood there, looking expectant and then disappointed. She reached back and press the flusher, and prayed.

"Can't a girl pee in peace?"

"I couldn't wait," he said, grabbed her and pulled her out of the bathroom and against the first horizontal surface, his office desk. He took the front of her shirt in both fists and ripped it open. She caught the vomit that rushed up her throat in her mouth.

"Hmm," he said.

"Excuse me?" she said.

"MMMMM. You look amazing. I think you were more fun fucked up, but you look better sober," he said his mouth on her throat, as he turned her around and bent her over the desk.

What happened next wasn't fun or even nostalgic, it felt like punishment. He was angry and trying not to show her, but Cora had been in this business long enough to know. She braced herself against the desk and her hands brushed papers that looked important. She tried to read them upside down. She studied the rest of the room. Maybe if she couldn't get them off her back with something on tape, maybe there was something that she could tell them about? She was memorizing the room and waiting for him to finish when she heard: "This isn't what I was expecting, at all."

She looked over her shoulder, Roy was standing in the doorway, a black wire and a dripping microphone dangling from his fingers. "Just trying to take a piss. Thought it was a black snake for a second. Made me jump a little, I'll admit." Her knees went out, she clung to the desk.

"Give me a second, would you?" Jackson grunted and Roy turned and left.

Jackson pressed her upper body hard into the desk. "You look scared," he said. "You should look scared. You didn't think you were getting away with anything, did you? You saw that truck, that TV? You've got to know I have a guy inside that joke of a police department. Someone who will tell me when some trash junkie is going to try to snitch on me?" He bit her shoulder as he came. His teeth tore her flesh. He put his hand on her lower back and held her there as he pulled up his pants. "You've always thought you were smarter than you are, Cora. It's been your downfall. Just stay down girl. Stay where you belong and you'll be just fine."

Cora gripped the edge of the desk. He was going to kill her.

"It's not mine," she said. "You know me. I grew up in front of you. You know I'm not a snitch." She worked hard to control her breathing. To not hyperventilate. To keep her voice even.

"I do know you. You're a cockroach. You'll do anything to survive. For a long time that worked in my favor." He turned her around, his big hand on her throat. "I bet your stomach smells like tape."

She swallowed hard. He laughed and pushed her out of the room, down the hall, and down the basement stairs into a room full of half stuffed animals. "You hang out down here in the dark with the rest of my toys while I figure out what to do with you," he said, then locked her in.

Cora searched the wall by the door for a light switch, when she finally found one it made a flick-flick sound as she flipped it, but nothing happened. She held her hands out in front of her, patting all manner of cold and sharp and cold and fuzzy things until she found a headlamp her must use for detail work. She turned it on and looked around. The room was full of Jackson's taxidermy projects and tools. The basement wasn't really finished. There were walls and a door, but the ceiling was open to the floor joists above. One entire wall was covered with pegboard, various saws hung on it. She shuddered. Dear god, she thought. Everything in that room was a weapon. There was a workbench and a tool box and a closet next to the door. No way out.

She could hear their voices through the floor.

"I really wanted to catch her wearing it." Jackson's voice was lower than Roy's.

"No matter," Roy said. "You know she's a snitch. This proves it. Not like you weren't going to kill her anyway."

She dug through the toolbox and found nothing good, only knives. When they came back for her, she wouldn't be able to get close enough to either of men to do any damage with a knife. She would be dead before she could get within feet if they even suspected she had something sharp. She searched again. The drawer at the bottom was locked with a combination. Cora hoped there was a gun. She tried Jackson's birthday, no luck. She couldn't remember his mama's birthday, but the day she died didn't work either. She didn't have time for this. She was ready to move on when she tried one more and it worked.

Cash's birthday. "Fuck," she said.

In the drawer she found a ring of keys, and a ledger book full of Jackson's scribbles, and a police badge. "Holy hell," she whispered. She wished desperately she had a pocket. She ran to the closet to see if there was anything she could wear and it was empty of clothes, but full of cardboard boxes. She ripped one open. Papers. And another, more papers. She didn't have time to open them all hoping for hoodie. Frustration ate at her. Not even a shitty old flannel. She squeezed her temples with her palms.

"I wanted to see the look on her face though. Her and that fucking brother of hers have been pain in my ass for so fucking long. Seeing her face when I ripped off the tape might have made some of it worth it," Jackson's voice was a bit muffled, but clear enough for her to hear his anger.

"That why you making her wait now?"

"Yeah. I want her to sweat. It's no fun to just shoot her. I want her to beg. Maybe I'll even get a nut in first since you interrupted the last one."

Cora's mouth was dry. Her heart raced. If she could get this stuff to the detective she was saved. She could start over with Cash. She would stop this fucking around and just go be him mom. He loved her. He'd always loved her. It was her own shit that was keeping her away. If they caught her with it, she knew, she was dead. But she was dead already, she reminded herself.

Cora walked the perimeter of the room like a caged tiger. She poked at random spots in the wall with a screwdriver looking for a soft spot. The floor was cement. The outside walls were cinderblock and solid. No windows. Her eyes kept going back to the unfinished ceiling. To those floor joists. To building projects with her own daddy, a perfectionist. But Jackson wasn't a perfectionist, she could see it in his taxidermy. He cut corners. He got lazy. She bet if he'd built this room for himself that there was a shortcut he'd taken, that she could use.

She was in the closet, rearranging boxes so she could see the back wall when she heard Roy: "ain't you gonna go deal with her?"

"What' the fucking rush? You got plans? Just go, I don't need you."

"I just don't like how quiet it is down there."

Cora wasn't sure what to do. Should she make noise, let them know that she was still down there? She kind of liked that she was freaking Roy out.

"It's fine," Jackson said. "She can't get out. I want her real desperate when I finally go down there."

She needed to work faster.

She moved box after cardboard box, but she finally found what she was looking for. Laziness. There was an air duct, and instead of doing it right, and cutting the shitty paneling that the walls were built out of to fit around the airduct and the floor joist, Jackson had left a hole. A hole that Cora was pretty sure she could get her hips through. Pretty sure. She made a staircase and a platform out of the boxes to get herself up to the hole. She stuck her head through, it was dark, but she could see that it was a straight drop to the floor on the other side. She had to make sure that she went straight down, or she was going to hit the furnace, and surely that would bring Jackson running. She had her lower body through the hole when she remembered the book, and the keys, and the badge. She wiggled back through and got them.

"She's mellowed," Roy said through the floor. "The Cora from before would have been screaming up a storm. It's fucking silent. I think you should be worried."

"Christ, get the fuck out of here, will you?" Jackson said. "I'm trying to rest up."

Cora heard footsteps cross the room, imagined Roy leaving and couldn't help and think that her chances just improved. But then she heard the basement door open and her heart stopped.

Roy's boots clomped down the stairs. Cora threw the book and the keys in the corner but hid the badge in her wild curly hair. She closed the closet doors, knelt beneath the workbench, and turned off the headlamp. For a long moment he paused outside the door and Cora waited in the dark, hoping that he'd change his mind. This room was a playground for a man like Roy.

He opened the door. She held her breath. The light switch flicked up and down, up and down. Roy cursed. He sucked his teeth and turned around, and turned all the lights in the hall on. The hall fixture lit a path into the room. Cora's hiding place was outside of the path. Roy walked in and put his hands on his hips. "I can smell you," he said. "Your cunt and your fear." He took two more steps toward her, cowboy boots echoing on the cement floor. She could see his face clearly. She could swear that he could see her in the dark, he was looking right at her, but he must have just been guessing. He rocked on his toes. "We been at this a long time, Cora. You've tied him up tighter than any woman, and I don't get it, but I don't question him. Surely, he's got his reasons. I had hoped when he was done with you that I'd have a chance to give you a try, to see what all the fuss is about, before he kills you, but that doesn't look like it's going to happen. I might have to settle for after. It's probably better for you that way, anyway."

Something crawled across Cora's neck, she wasn't sure if it was a spider or her revulsion. She tried to breathe quieter, to make her heart beat quieter, to silence her thoughts as if she could tell where she was in the room from the screams in her head.

He sniffed and stepped closer.

She tried to make herself smaller.

He sniffed and stepped closer again. Now he was outside of the pool of light too, and Cora could only make out the shape of him, all old twigs and rubber bands. One more step. Now she could touch him, or worse, he, her. She held her breath.

He squatted and faced her like he knew where she was all along. "Maybe he wouldn't mind," he whispered. "Maybe he wouldn't have to know."

"I'd tell him," she said.

"Not without your tongue," Roy said, snapping his teeth. Faster than she thought possible he pulled her from beneath the bench and straddling her, held her hands above her head. Roy pressed them painfully into the rough concrete of the floor. Cora managed to push out one shriek before he covered her mouth with his. But that one was enough to notify Jackson that his property was being sullied and for Jackson to holler "Roy" from the living room.

Roy sighed. "Be right back, Baby," he said, leaving the room, closing the door, and bringing the darkness back.

Cora didn't have a minute to spare. As she climbed the boxes in the closet the badge fell out of her hair. She couldn't lose it. She put it in her mouth. She slithered her legs back through the hole and then squeezed her ass and hips through. Her skin was raw with scrapes from the edge of the paneling and full of splinters from the floor joist. Once the majority of her weight was through the gap she had a decision to make. She couldn't really hold on any longer, she needed to make her shoulders smaller to fit through, but she also wasn't looking forward to how falling over the edge was going to feel on her breasts. She attempted to brace herself against the ceiling, and slide her boobs through, but when gravity finally got her, she was sure she'd left the right one behind, attached to the top of the paneling. She landed on the concrete floor on her ass, and the badge made her mouth bleed, but she was out of the terrifying room.

She surveyed her options. The basement was a walkout. Thank heavens they lived in the mountains and no one lived on a level lot. Cora nearly cried with relief, and then cried again when she couldn't get the slider to open more than two inches. She searched to see if he'd put some kind of stopper in the track, or if there was a lock that she couldn't see, but it was just a shitty door, and she wasn't strong enough. She was going to have to break it, but that would end her advantage. Jackson and Roy would be here in moments; she needed a plan. She scoured the basement for the things she could use, and sent a prayer to a god she was sure that she stopped believing in when her mama and daddy died, and the piece of shit drunk who hit them didn't.

A golfclub broke the window, and knocked out enough of the glass that she could get through. She threw an old doormat over the opening so she could climb through in her bare feet. Sprinkles of glass shimmered all over her body in the yard when Jackson turned his floodlight on and hollered at her from the back deck. It was only the rack of the shotgun that mattered, she wasn't waiting around to see if he'd use it. She didn't know where Roy was.

"You ain't gonna get far naked," he said. "I'mma right behind you."

If Jackson figured her nudity would be impediment to her escape, he was wrong. He should know she didn't care who saw her naked. Hell, even if she didn't sell her services to survive, childbirth alone would have stolen all of her dignity. It had felt like the whole town had been there to watch her poop on the table. Every woman in town had had her hands on Cora's tits trying to help her nurse fussy Cash. Her body basically belonged to the town. Wasn't the female body public property?

Cora ran through the woods, branches tearing at her, roots tripping her. The thumping of her heart kept her from being able to hear the critters, the ruffling of leaves, and the slithering against the underbrush and she was happy for that. Something big landed on her shoulder and when she brushed it off it mushed in her hand and she nearly screamed. But then she remembered what was behind her was much, much worse.

Eventually she came to a road, and she ran down the side, gravel slicing her feet, hoping that maybe she could flag down a ride, but she walked for miles before she saw anything other than road. When a chicken barn materialized, she realized that she'd been walking in the wrong direction, away from town and the bridge of her nose started to pinch and ache. She ran to the door trying not to hope that it was open and there was someone inside who could help. But the door was locked, and even after she banged on it like a madwoman all she could hear was the whirr of the fans and the occasional cluck. There was no one. Cora leaned against the building and cried. Then, she wondered what time it was and when the employees would start to arrive. She walked around the barn looking for another way in, but the backdoor was locked too. She was looking for somewhere to take cover until the workers arrived, when she saw the bicycle with a basket and then she laughed at the joke that the universe was playing on her.

It took a long time.

She took the back roads, and had to ditch every time she saw headlights, twice she saw Roy's truck and threw up, but she made it to Lee's and mercifully he was alone, and had left the door unlocked. She grabbed some clothes and put the badge in her record case and locked it. The badge was everything she needed to start over. She'd done it. She couldn't hardly believe it. She was going to be able to clear herself. She was going to be able to face Chuck and Cash free from her past and ready to move forward together. She was in the shower cleaning her wounds when Lee came in and sat on the toilet.

"Where you been," he said from the other side of the curtain.

"It's better you don't know."

"Police came by a couple of hours ago."

"I expect they did."

"You really not going to tell me?"

"Cause you've been so forthcoming?" she slid open the shower curtain and reached for a towel.

"Holy shit, you're hurt. You've got to go to the hospital."

"I'm fine. I got something to do first. And then I'll have all the time in the world for the hospital."

She put on her clothes and used his hair brush and deodorant.

"Can I borrow your truck?"

"What for?"

"Got to go to the police station."

"The cop who came here said you shouldn't go in. Said you should just call and he'd come get you. He was actually pretty adamant that you didn't go in, said it wasn't safe. He left his card. Hold on."

Lee came back with a card and handed it to her.

"Cutsforth," she said. "Fuck me," she said and sat down on the toilet.

"You going to call him?"

"He's Jackson's," she said bending over and resting her elbows on her knees, her face in her hands. She wondered if the detective was too, there was no way to know. Had the whole thing been a way for Jackson to kill her? Was getting Cash back ever even an option? It was all for nothing. She stood for a long time looking at herself in the mirror. "Take me to my brother's?"

Lee nodded.

They didn't talk on the way to Chuck's. When they pulled into the driveway Lee put his hand over hers. Cora looked at the house that she grew up in. The house that had felt less and less like her home with every bump, with every needle. Her son was in there sleeping safely. She could go in and they would take her in, but then tomorrow night when her son was sleeping, he wouldn't be safe. She was a walking catastrophe, and as much as she wanted to be with family, to not be alone, to stop this constant wandering, she couldn't destroy them to comfort herself. "Actually, could you take me to Dottie's?"

"If you need something I've got a joint."

"It's not that," she said shaking her head and then leaning it on the glass of the passenger door. He backed out and drove up the mountain. When they got to the driveway marked with the hub cap she had him stop and let her out.

"Bye," she said.

"I didn't mean for—"

"Doesn't matter," she said, and it didn't. It was always going to come to this.

The sun was coming up as she climbed the cinder blocks to Dottie's door. She didn't bother knocking. In the trailer Dottie laid on the couch watching TV that sat on the floor. "Hey," she said but didn't move.

"I need you to keep this for me," Cora said. "Don't give it to anyone but Chuck, and only do that if you think I'm dead." She put the record case on the floor and put the TV on top of it and walked out.

Acknowledgments

These stories record a long journey, from my first foray into publishing in 2016 with "Porch Light Salvation" to my most recent in 2022's: "And Then the Forest Will Burn Down." They mark big wins and broken hearts, and so many lessons learned. But one thing is constant, while all of the mistakes are my own, these stories would not have been possible without the help of many incredibly generous people, whom I owe much more than thanks.

Firstly, to Ron Earl Phillips, the only publisher I considered for this collection, who saw my vision and made it better.

To the writers who blurbed this collection: Nathan Ballingrud, Peter Farris, Gabino Iglesias, Laura McHugh, Brian Panowich, Steph Post, J. Todd Scott, and George Singleton, who buoyed me through the swamping tsunami of imposter syndrome, who are not only my influences and heroes as brilliant writers, but as deeply kind and thoughtful people (please readers, buy their books).

To my friends: Charlotte Hamrick, Ed Karshner, Emry Trantham, Kathleen Calby, Karen Luke Jackson, Vern Smith, Charlie Wilkinson, C.W. Blackwell, Rob Smith, Dawn Harris, Allison Brown, Brad Proctor, Jason Grell, M. Scott Douglass, Laurel Hightower, Eve Webb, Bobby Mathews, and George

Wood, who have been so generous with their time, advice, patience, and bourbon.

To Chris and Eon at City Lights Books in Sylva, NC who go above and beyond for small press authors.

To my family and cheerleaders at Gold Leaf Literary for making me look good.

Special thanks to the Good Hart Artist Residency, Bill and Sue Klco, Harbor Springs Festival of the Book, Amy Gillard, Robert Morris University, Dr. Heather Pinson, Dr. Edward Karshner, Dr. Sylvia Pamboukian, Dr. Jon Radermacher, and Dr. Frank Hartle, for the gift of time and financial support.

To Brodie and Redding, no matter what I write, you'll always be my best work.

To Josh, who knows my heart, and loves me anyway.

*M*EAGAN LUCAS is the author of the award-winning novel, *Songbirds and Stray Dogs* (Main Street Rag Press, 2019). Meagan has published over 30 short stories and essays in journals like *Still: The Journal*, *Cowboy Jamboree*, *BULL*, *Pithead Chapel*, and others. She is Pushcart, Best of the Net, Derringer, and Canadian Crime Writer's Award of Excellence nominated, and won the 2017 Scythe Prize for Fiction. Her novel *Songbirds and Stray Dogs* was chosen to represent North Carolina in the Library of Congress 2022 Route 1 Reads program. Meagan teaches Creative Writing at Robert Morris University. She is the Editor in Chief of *Reckon Review*. Born and raised on a small island in Northern Ontario, she now lives in the mountains of Western North Carolina.

About
Shotgun Honey Books

Thank you for reading *Here in the Dark* by Meagan Lucas.

Shotgun Honey began as a crime genre flash fiction webzine in 2011 created as a venue for new and established writers to experiment in the confines of a mere 700 words. More than a decade later, Shotgun Honey still challenges writers with that storytelling task, but also provides opportunities to expand beyond through our book imprint and has since published anthologies, collections, novellas and novels by new and emerging authors. We hope you have enjoyed this book. That you will share your experience, review and rate this title positively on your favorite book review sites and with your social media family and friends.

Visit ShotgunHoneyBooks.com

SHOTGUN HONEY

FICTION WITH A KICK

shotgunhoneybooks.com

CPSIA information can be obtained
at www.ICGtesting.com
Printed in the USA
BVHW031149290623
666566BV00005B/11